PRAISE FOR
GIFT FROM THE STARS

"A novel with spirited characters who inspire a renewed love of one's own kind. Highly recommended as adventure and therapy for pessimists."

GEORGE ZEBROWSKI
Campbell Prize-winning author of *Brute Orbits*

⊨

"*Gift from the Stars* is an imaginative story of First Contact, told from a very human point of view. It begins in an unassuming used bookstore and expands relentlessly outward to encompass some of the most exciting speculations in cosmology."

ROBERT J. SCHERRER
Chair, Department of Physics and Astronomy,
Vanderbilt University

— JAMES GUNN —

GIFT
from the
STARS

BENBELLA BOOKS, INC.
Dallas, Texas

BenBella Books, Inc.
6440 N. Central Expressway, Suite 617
Dallas, TX 75206
www. benbellabooks. com
Send feedback to feedback@benbellabooks.com

PUBLISHER: Glenn Yeffeth
EDITOR: Shanna Caughey
ASSOCIATE EDITOR: Leah Wilson
DIRECTOR OF MARKETING/PR: Laura Watkins

Printed in the United States of America
10 9 8 7 6 5 4 3 2 1

Library of Congress Cataloging-in-Publication Data
Gunn, James, 1923–
   Gift from the stars / by James Gunn.
     p. cm.
   ISBN 1-932100-65-2
   1. Human-alien encounters—Fiction. I. Title.

PS3557. U4858G54 2005
813'. 6--dc22

                                                        2005002701

Cover photo courtesy of NASA
Cover design by Melody Cadungog
Text design and composition by John Reinhardt Book Design

Distributed by Independent Publishers Group
To order call (800) 888-4741
www. ipgbook. com

For special sales contact Laura Watkins at laura@benbellabooks. com

This novel is dedicated to my indispensable advisors on matters scientific and speculative:

Adrian Melott, Philip Baringer and Robert Scherrer

ACKNOWLEDGMENTS

"The Giftie" was published in *Analog,* September 1999

"Pow'r" was published in *Analog,* January 2000

"The Abyss" was published in *Analog,* July/August 2000

"The Rabbit Hole" was published in *Analog,* December 2001

"Uncreated Night and Strange Shadows" was published,
in somewhat different form, in *Analog,* January/February 2005

CONTENTS

PREFACE

IN 1972 SCRIBNERS PUBLISHED A NOVEL of mine called *The Listeners*. Scribners' promotion director sent out galleys to a number of authors and scientists, and, among others, Carl Sagan was kind enough to read them and offer a quote: "One of the very best fictional portrayals of contact with extra-terrestrial intelligence ever written." It was used as an above-the-title blurb on every edition published after Sagan became even better known when he created his popular-astronomy television show *Cosmos* in 1980.

The following year Sagan signed a contract with Simon & Schuster to write a science-fiction novel called *Contact*. It was finally published in 1985.

When the film version of *Contact* finally was released in 1997 (delayed even more than the writing of the novel), my reaction was mixed: I enjoyed the film and yet I felt that it was romantic rather than realistic. The novel *Contact* had portrayed working scientists realistically and the film perhaps a bit less so, but the plans transmitted were fantastic and the method and purpose of the space journey, not only fantastic but a letdown (a common fault of sf novels). And the question of why aliens would send the plans was never adequately explored.

That isn't the way it would happen, I told myself, and I was "inspired" to write *Gift from the Stars*, a response not only to *Contact* but to every novel of humans encountering the unknown. I wrote it as a series of novelettes, just as I had written *The Listeners*, and published them over a period of half a dozen years in *Analog*, beginning with "The Giftie," which won the *Analog* readers' poll for best novelette of the year. I have kept that pattern in the book, even though I planned it from the beginning as a novel exploring "the way it would really be." It is a novel in six parts instead of a dozen or so chapters.

If aliens sent us plans for a spaceship, the novel suggests, they would arrive without fanfare and their arrival would be greeted not with surprise or joy or gratitude, but with suspicion and resistance. A few space enthusiasts would want to implement them to reach the stars, but the great masses of humanity—and the bureaucrats who make decisions for them—would ignore the plans or want to suppress them. Most of all, why would aliens send us spaceship plans? Are their intentions beneficent or inimical? Damon Knight raised the question in a classic short-short story entitled "To Serve Man," but *Gift from the Stars* pursues the question in detail and arrives at an answer, like the spaceship the humans construct and name *Ad Astra Per Aspera*. "To the stars through difficulty."

Gift from the Stars is a more light-hearted look at the issues of alien contact—the plans, for instance, are discovered as an appendix in a book on a UFO remainder table—and I enjoyed writing them and living with the characters: Adrian Mast, Frances Farmstead, Jessica Buhler, and the troubled genius Peter Cavendish. I liked Frances so much I couldn't bear to let her die from old age before the novel was over, so I invented a rejuvenation process. I hope you enjoy them as much.

JAMES GUNN
Lawrence, Kansas

Introduction

LOOKING WITH A WIDE EYE

JAMES GUNN HAS PRESIDED over his distinguished career with a skeptical and insightful eye. More to the point, that eye has seen longer in time and wider in ideas than most of his peers'.

Gift from the Stars is a good example. This ingenious tale starts with what seems a rank implausibility—a Big Idea carried in a UFO book, of all things. Then it propagates forward, doubling the scale of thought with each new novelette-length piece. The structure—which writers notice immediately but readers mostly take for granted, like rafters plunging down whitewater rapids—reminds me of A. E. van Vogt, who once told me his method of building long tales, all the way up to novels, lay in introducing a new idea every eight hundred words.

In van Vogt this process led to gathering incoherence. In Gunn, to expansive vistas.

Rereading van Vogt, I feel the whitewater rapids effect again. With Gunn, an expanding vision.

I'm not going to give away the plot turns and swerves in this novel, lest I steal from you the pleasures of it. Gunn has elected to tell his tale in his usual direct, clear prose, and the ideas unfold with the same precision.

Instead, let me hark back to an earlier high point in his career, *The Listeners*. It, too, views alien intelligences through the lens of humans' own struggles. In *The Listeners* we follow scientists confronting the ultimate hope of the Search for Extraterrestrial Intelligence, SETI—a signal from afar. That 1960s novel came well before Carl Sagan's *Contact*, and Sagan clearly took much from *The Listeners*. Seldom do sf writers get judged by how their ideas have played out in reality, yet it is a useful standard.

So...how have Gunn's ideas fared since then?

I have been close to the SETI Institute for decades and know the principals there well. I think they haven't been playing enough attention to Jim Gunn.

There are reasons to believe that we may be missing an opportunity in SETI research by ignoring some classes of Beacons—those big, bright, occasional broadcasts that our current SETI program has little chance of seeing. Why?

Beacons built by distant, advanced and wealthy societies may have very different characteristics from what SETI researchers have been looking for. The targets of most SETI searches are radio-transmitting societies intent on communicating a message to us. Most of these SETI searches have looked at stars a few hundred light years from ours.

That's a tiny neighborhood. We know that star formation started at the Galactic Center about ten billion years ago. This means that metals built up early from the supernovas there, so planets capable of sustaining interesting organic life could have begun their slow winding path upward toward life and intelligence within the first billion or so years. A world like ours, that took 4.5 billion years to produce technological intelligence, would have done so near the Galactic Center about four billion years ago.

In that much time, intelligence might have lapsed, arisen again, or gotten inconceivably rich. The beyond-all-reckoning wealthy aliens near the Center could afford to lavish a pittance blaring their presence out to all.

As Gunn said in *The Listeners*, motivation influences search strategy.

Thinking broadly, high-power transmitters might be built for a wide variety of reasons. Here is a list of a few that occurred to me:

Leakage Radiation: Here we don't refer to the usual meaning, of commercial radio and television broadcasts irradiating isotropically. There are possible applications for some extremely high power transmitters: deep space radar, and the beaming of energy over solar system distances, as an advanced spacefaring society might use. There's also the possibility of driving interstellar starships with beams of lasers, millimeter or microwaves. Such beams would be coherent but carry no message. They could also be pulsed, not continuous.

Ozymandias (from the poem by Shelley): Here the motivation in sheer pride; the beacon announces the existence of a high civilization—a brag. A message may or may not be encoded.

Help!: Quite possibly societies that plan over time scales ~1000 years will foresee physical problems and wish to discover if others have surmounted them. An example is a civilization whose star is warming (as ours is), and who may wish to move their planet outward with gravitational tugs. Many others are possible.

The Funeral Pyre: Suppose help doesn't come. A civilization near the end of its life simply announces its existence to the universe by constructing a large high-power transmitter built to last eons. Emphasis could be on the power radiated and not on any particular message content. There are many ways to clearly indicate that a signal is artificial without having to encode complex information. Recall that the pyramids carry no written messages but many implied ones. This might be a howl of despair, hurled out to the unfeeling stars. There have been stranger human monuments....

SETI Correspondents: This is what SETI researchers are listening for—civilizations that wish to communicate. The message is highly encoded and has a very narrow band to facilitate reception.

We might find any of these. James Gunn picked one—the Funeral Pyre—and made an eloquent drama of it.

The SETI theorists have certainly been influenced by his work. I spoke of this to Jill Tarter and Frank Drake, the gray wise heads of the Institute, and they both remembered *The Listeners* immediately.

Alas, little consideration has been given to the physical limitations the Beacon-builder faces in constructing extremely high power radiators. The implications for what signals should look like *in general* are unstudied. Up to now, SETI research has been conducted from the point of view of *receivers*, not *transmitters*.

Here's where my own research interests come into play. Our understanding of very high power devices developed over the last thirty years on Earth is that they have very different characteristics from the types of transmitters SETI is looking for at present. One major difference is that the highest power systems (peak powers over ten gigawatt—a billion watts) trade off peak power for average power, in order to get to a much stronger signal at long distance, at the lowest cost. They are pulsed because of requirements for heating and cooling. Broadcasting generates lots of waste heat!

Most of these devices are not extremely narrow band—whereas your own cell phone, for example, works well because it is narrow band in frequency. For fundamental physics reasons, their bandwidths are much higher than the one-Hz span of SETI receivers.

In other words, the big broadcasters don't look at all like the sorts of transmitters that the SETI programs have assumed would be built.

This means we may be looking for the wrong kind of steady, stable hail from a distant star.

This idea is only now gathering strength within the SETI community.

But Jim Gunn thought of it long ago. In *The Listeners* scientists find a beacon and its melancholy message. He got it right.

So it is with *Gift from the Stars*. Lively, intense, it holds a wealth of good ideas. Gunn's aptly named Enigmatics are odd indeed, with motivations more strange than the ideas I gave above about SETI beacons.

Perhaps—I hope!—we will not have to wait forty years to see them bear fruit.

GREGORY BENFORD
February 2005

O wad some Pow'r the giftie gie us
To see oursels as others see us!

⊢⊣

Part One

THE GIFTIE

IT ALL STARTED AT THE LITTLE BOOKSTORE where Adrian liked to browse when he had the time. Browsing in the chain superstores wasn't the same. In the superstores you could find almost any kind of book you wanted, and anything you couldn't find could be located by computer and made available a day or so later. That was assuming you knew what you wanted, or could find it in the current maze of instant literature. But there were so many books that you couldn't *browse* in an eclectic jumble of old and new. Anyway, the superstores didn't *smell* right. They smelled like, well, like department stores with air recirculated every thirty seconds. Bookstores should smell like old leather and good paper and printer's ink and maybe a little dust.

The book was on a table labeled "Remainders—Cults, New Age, UFOs." The books had once been stacked neatly—the proprietor of the Book Nook, a Mrs. Frances Farmstead of elderly years, but with a youthful devotion to books nourished by some sixty years of reading and handling, liked them arranged so that all the bindings could be read at a glance—but now they were jumbled in a heap as if someone else had already rummaged through them.

That honed Adrian's edge of irritation over his inability to get any closer to the goal he had been pursuing since childhood, ever since he had looked up at the stars and, like John Carter, had wished himself among them. The feeling of irritation had been growing in recent months. His ambition to be an astronaut had been grounded by the in-arguable fact that he was physically unimposing, and his poor hand-eye coordination had always made him last to be chosen at pick-up games. But he had a nimble and inquiring mind, and he had settled for the next best thing: aerospace engineering.

He had worked his way through university, joined a major aerospace firm after graduation, and resigned after a dozen years of routine assign-ments that got him no closer to his goal of reaching the stars, through surrogates if not in person. He had set up a consulting business, and was able to pick and choose assignments that appealed to him and seemed to get humanity closer to freedom from Earth's gravity. But even sec-ond-hand space adventuring was hung up on chemical propulsion and obsolete vehicles. His own ambition, like the space program itself, was drifting. Humanity needed something totally new. The irritation had brought him into the Book Nook time and again; browsing had proved, over the years, a treatment if not a cure. But now someone else might have found the one text the book gods had intended for him, for which their mysterious hands had guided him into the store. These remainders were all one of a kind, and once one was removed it was gone forever. Ordinarily he would not have chosen this particular table—he had a skeptic's fondness for books whose naive pretensions or paranoid con-spiracies he could ridicule to his friends or even to himself—but he was not in the mood for such cynical amusements. The jumble attracted him, however, and he worked his way through the pile, restacking them neatly on the table, binding up, in the way Mrs. Farmstead would have done herself. *The UFO Conspiracy, UFOs: The Final Answer, UFO: The Complete Sightings*, and *Cosmic Voyage*, along with *The Secret Doctrine of the Rosicrucians, The Truth in the Light, Psychic Animals*, and other an-nals of magic and the occult. Adrian could feel Mrs. Farmstead's approv-ing gaze from the antique wooden desk at the front of the store.

He held a book in his hand, turning it this way and that. The book had lost its dust jacket, if it ever had one, but it had a pleasant feel to it, and the title was catchy: *Gift from the Stars*. Perhaps it was a Von Dan-iken clone; he always enjoyed their innocent credulity. He opened it. The book had a frontispiece, unusual in a cheap text like this. It showed the vast metal bowl of the radio telescope at Arecibo, with the focusing mechanism held aloft by cables strung from three pylons. The title page listed a publisher he had never heard of, but that wasn't unusual: fringe publishers were common in the cult field. The copyright page said that the book had been published half a dozen years earlier. Adrian glanced at the first page. It was the usual stuff: have we been visited? Are there aliens among us?

He leafed through the book, half decided to put it down, when he came across an appendix filled with diagrams. Not diagrams of cryptic incisions on arid plateaus in Peru or carved around the entrances to ancient tombs. These seemed to be designs for some kind of ship. Not "some kind of ship," he decided with the gathering excitement he recognized as the eureka feeling, but a spaceship, and not the sketchy drawings of some putative crashed UFO concealed in a hangar in New Mexico or Dayton, but engineering drawings such as Adrian worked with almost every day. He took it to the desk.

"Found something you like, Mr. Mast?" Mrs. Farmstead asked. She was old but cheerful about it, with a plump, grandmotherly face and gray hair braided and wound into a knot pinned on top of her head with an oversized barrette.

"Enough to pay good money for it," Adrian said. Mrs. Farmstead didn't accept charge cards, but she had been known to run an account for someone short on cash who had fallen in love with a book. "Any idea where it came from?"

"Of course I do," Mrs. Farmstead said. She maintained careful records that kept her in the shop, Adrian suspected, long after the time of its official closing. "But you don't expect me to look them up for a three-fifty remaindered title, do you, Mr. Mast?" Her sharp glance over plastic-rimmed glasses dared him to ask for special service.

"Not this time, Mrs. Farmstead," he said, paid his money, and took his hand-written receipt and his newfound treasure and walked out of the store, feeling no longer irritated but elated, almost trembling, as if what he had found there would change his life forever.

————

Nobody was dependent on him except those space travelers not yet liberated from the surly bonds of the Solar System, perhaps not yet born; for a dream he had sacrificed hopes for wife and family. Who was he kidding? His problem was that the women he was interested in weren't interested in him, and the ones who were interested in him he found less exciting than his work. Ordinarily, then, there was nothing to draw him back to his one-bedroom apartment, but now a curious anticipation hastened his step.

He delayed gratification by changing into comfortable sweat pants, getting a cold can of beer from the refrigerator and a bottle of peanuts from the pantry, and settled into his easy chair in the living room opposite the television set he turned on only for the news, the science channels and the sci-fi series. Only then did he open his *Gift from the Stars*.

The first chapter was titled "Where Are They?" Although it seemed to be a discussion of aliens and the possibility that they might have visited the earth in ages past and even might be keeping track of us now, Adrian recognized a subtext the ordinary reader would never have noticed. A conclusion seemed to say that evidence of alien visitation may have been deliberately concealed by nameless government agencies, but that other alien contacts had occurred, or were yet to happen, that anyone with an eye to the sky or a mind to understand could be aware of. Read with greater sophistication, however, the chapter suggested that the evidence for alien visitation was not only thin but probably nothing more than the connecting of random dots; that aliens were the modern equivalent of angels and demons; and that belief in alien visitation and abduction was a substitute for antiquated religions, whose answers no longer seemed appropriate to contemporary questions.

Between the lines, however, Adrian detected an argument for the existence of aliens. Logic said that with all the stars in the Milky Way galaxy alone, a good number of them would nourish life and a good number of those would develop technological civilizations capable of interstellar travel. Good scientists had agreed on all that. Surely there must be aliens older, wiser, and more advanced than humanity. But, as Fermi asked, where are they? Why aren't they here by now?

The UFO believers, of course, thought they were here, observing us, maybe abducting people for their experiments, maybe having accidents that left their spaceship wreckage and alien bodies strewn across remote areas of the world to be hidden by government agencies concerned about popular panic or paranoid about alien takeovers, or committed to their own research and fearful of the release of dangerous information.... But *Gift from the Stars* suggested, subtly, that aliens had their own reasons for not visiting Earth, reasons that we could never know, unless, perhaps, we should go visit *them*.

The question Adrian had to answer was more immediate: why should the book he held in his hands be titled and written in such a way that it was virtually indistinguishable from a hundred, maybe a thousand, other books on UFOs and aliens? The only reason he could think of was that the author wanted to hide a message that would be found only by someone capable of noticing and understanding it. Like concealing a diamond in a heap of glass imitations. What better hiding place for obscure revelations than among the books that the only people who would take them seriously were the people that nobody took seriously?

Unable to restrain his impatience any longer, he turned to the appendix. Here were the drawings he remembered. They could be for any kind of vehicle, a submarine, say, or an airplane without wings, but the design had non-aerodynamic extensions as if intended for use where fluid resistance was non-existent. The drawings were curiously uneven as if they had been prepared by some gross process different from the customary draftsman lines. Gaps in the drawings seemed to indicate details yet to be added or filled in according to individual preferences. But Adrian identified what was clearly a propulsion system based upon the reaction mass being expelled through nozzles at the rear of the vessel. The storage space for fuel seemed too small, however, and the reaction chamber itself seemed oddly shaped and also curiously small.

Adrian turned more pages. The book had a second appendix in which he discovered the design for an engine in which two substances would be combined and the energy obtained used to accelerate another substance through oddly shaped nozzles and past some kind of magnetic fields until it was released. A final sketch made sense of the limited storage space and the engine. It was a design for a container in which the substance within would never touch the sides. The substance was a plasma contained by magnetic fields maintained by some kind of permanent magnets built into the vessel, or perhaps the vessel itself was magnetic. A companion design showed how solar energy could be transformed into—what else could it be?—antimatter. Its combination with matter—perhaps hydrogen encountering anti-hydrogen—would convert the mass of both entirely into energy and provide the means by which humanity could reach the stars.

Would it work? Somehow he doubted it. It was all too pat, like a science-fiction gadget. But maybe that's what all advanced technology looked like—not magic but obvious. And, like a cultist's scenario, it all made sense, granted the premise, and was not that much different from imaginative concepts discussed in aerospace engineering circles. The difference was that these looked as if they were working designs, not concepts, and even, somehow, as if they were antiquated, like museum pieces or redesigns of historic airships such as the Wright brothers' first craft. It would work, all right, probably better than the original, but it hinted at the existence of methods far more effective. Were those beyond the understanding or the technological capabilities of less-advanced species?

Adrian shook his head. He was allowing his imagination to take him into theories as weird as those of any UFO true believer. But that was what the book had done to him: he had picked it up as a minor contribution to a neurotic belief system and it had evolved into a document addressing his deepest needs. And, although the text did not say so, the title suggested that somehow these designs had come from somewhere else, perhaps from aliens. Perhaps they were, indeed, a gift from the stars.

———

Adrian showed the book to Mrs. Farmstead. "You said you could tell me where this came from."

"Yes," she said, peering up at him owlishly over her glasses, her plump face framed in coils of gray. "But surely one of these is enough." She looked at his face as if reading his need. "Oh, all right, since it's you, Mr. Mast." She ran a handheld optical scanner across the ISBN number on the title page and then punched a couple of keys on her computer. "It arrived six months ago in a box of remainders from a jobber. Cheap."

"All cult books?"

"Most of them, I expect."

"Could we find out who wrote it?"

She pointed at the name on the title page: George Winterbotham.

"Could you find an address for him?" Adrian asked. He apologized. "I know this is a lot of trouble."

Mrs. Farmstead seemed about to say something but instead turned back to the computer and called up *Books in Print*. Nothing. She tried several library databases, including the Library of Congress. Nothing. She laughed. "This may be the only copy in existence." ·

Adrian grimaced. "That may be more accurate than you think."

She looked at him. "What are we doing here, Mr. Mast? Is it illegal?"

"It may be dangerous," he replied, only half in jest, "but it's not illegal unless it is illegal to publish a book revealing information that some people might want withheld."

"Trade secrets?" she asked. "In that?"

He had hoped to keep Mrs. Farmstead out of it. Something about this situation had a wrongness to it—the information that should not be in a book like this, the accidental way it came into his hands, the curious anonymity of its author. He flipped the book open to its appendices. "There are these," he said. "They're spaceship designs."

"How do you know?"

"You know books. I know spaceships," he said. "I don't think I've ever introduced myself: I'm an aerospace engineer. I work in designs like these."

"How very odd," she said and leafed through the appendices. Her expression told him they meant nothing to her. "I'll take your word for it."

"I'd like to find the author and ask him where he got the designs."

"I see," Mrs. Farmstead said. "But why would he publish them in a book like this?"

"Exactly," Adrian said. "It suggests that he wanted someone to find them, someone who would understand what they were—"

"Like you, Mr. Mast?"

He nodded. "And nobody else would know they were there, particularly nobody who might want to keep them from the public."

"And that nobody, or even a group of nobodies, might be dangerous to someone who found out what they didn't want found out."

"I'm afraid so, Mrs. Farmstead."

"Well," she said and turned back to her computer. "I don't like people who want to keep things from being published." She tapped several keys. " We can look up the publisher."

The publisher, at least, was listed on the Internet. He had two books under his name, both UFO texts. Neither one was *Gift from the Stars*. Before Adrian could stop Mrs. Farmstead, she had typed in a telephone number. Somewhere a phone started ringing.

"Hello?" she said into a speaker so that Adrian could hear. "Is this Joel Simpson? The publisher?"

"Yes," came the hesitant reply. "Who's calling?"

"I have a customer who is trying to find another copy of a book published by you half a dozen years ago."

"I've only published two books," Simpson said.

Mrs. Farmstead raised her eyebrows at Adrian as if to say, "He's lying."

"*Gift from the Stars.*"

"There must be some mistake. I never published a book by that title," the voice on the other end said. "Who is calling?"

"Sorry for the trouble," Mrs. Farmstead said. "It must have been another publisher with the same name." She pressed a button that closed the connection. "Well, Mr. Mast? You may be right."

"I wish you hadn't made that call," Adrian said. "I have a feeling that somebody got to Mr. Simpson and scared him into suppressing the book and reporting anybody who inquired about it. Maybe this *is* the only copy."

"I never told him my name."

"There's such a thing as caller ID and even tapped telephone lines."

"I never thought of that," she said. "The way you talk about it, it sounds like some kind of conspiracy."

"I hope I'm wrong," he said. "I hope I haven't been reading too many of those cult conspiracy books."

"No matter," she said, her plump face tightening into a look of determination, "we're going to get to the bottom of this, no matter what."

"We seem to have run into a brick wall," Adrian said.

"There are ways around a wall," she said darkly. "As you said, Mr. Mast, books are my business. Just give me a few hours with this computer, and I'll find the author for you—or, at least, where we can locate the author."

"We, Mrs. Farmstead?"

"I told you that I don't like people who want to keep things from being published," she said. "I don't like people who threaten other people, either."

"I won't turn down your help," Adrian said. "But I never intended drawing you into this."

"I am in, Mr. Mast," she said, "and unless you forbid me from helping, we're in this together. But tell me: what is it we're trying to do?"

"We're trying to discover where these designs came from and whether there are more of them," Adrian said. "And then we're going to build a spaceship and go to the stars."

"That's worth taking a few risks for," she said. "I've always wanted to go to the stars." She turned back to her computer.

That night the Book Nook burned down.

———

Next morning they traveled stand-by to Phoenix. Adrian paid for the tickets with cash that he had withdrawn from an ATM, but he had to give their real names to the young woman who sold him the tickets and demanded photo ID. He had tried to persuade Mrs. Farmstead not to go along, but she was determined.

"Your bookstore has just been burned," Adrian said. "Somebody doesn't want us to follow this up."

They were sitting in the coach section, Mrs. Farmstead in the window seat, Adrian in the seat next to her, leaving the aisle seat empty. They had their heads close together like conspirators.

"Nonsense!" Mrs. Farmstead said. "The building was nearly one hundred years old, and the wiring was almost as old. It was an accident waiting to happen."

"But right after your telephone call?"

"People have a dangerous tendency to connect events, Mr. Mast—"

"Call me Adrian," he said.

"All right," she said, "and you can call me Mrs. Farmstead." She looked at him over the tops of her glasses and smiled. "Misconnecting events is what's wrong with UFO fanatics. They get cause and effect all mixed up. Just because two events happen, one following the other or next to the other, doesn't mean they're related. *Ad hoc propter hoc*, it's called."

"So you think—?"

"Coincidence," she said. "That means 'happening together.' I've spent a lot of time with dictionaries. I like words, Adrian, and I think they need respect." They were passing over southwest Kansas with its circular green patches below attesting to the existence of central-pivot irrigation. "Now that's cause and effect, Adrian," she said, pointing out the window beside her. "Like the book that has sent us off on this adventure. Either those drawings are intended to make otherwise unlikely comments seem more believable—"

"Not that, Mrs. Farmstead," Adrian said. "I know legitimate designs when I see them."

"Or, as you suspect, someone has tried to hide a golden acorn on the forest floor."

"That's a good image, Mrs. Farmstead. Only"—he hesitated—"this may be dangerous business." He held up a hand to stop her response. "I know: you think recent events are unrelated, and that there's no danger from people who don't want that acorn found. You may be right. But you may be wrong, and you shouldn't have to take that chance."

"At my age, you mean?" she said.

"At any age. You should be home taking care of cleaning up the site of your store, or collecting your insurance."

"And sitting in my rocking chair?"

"Rebuilding. Restocking. Whatever."

"I don't choose to retire and, to tell you the truth, I was getting a little bored with the book business. People don't buy good books anymore. Hardly any books at all to tell the full story. Maybe the fire was a blessing in disguise. It may have liberated me to do something important, like giving humanity the stars."

"That's eloquent, Mrs. Farmstead," Adrian said.

"Besides, as you said, your area is spaceships. Mine is books. How far do you think you'd have got looking for spaceships?"

He thought about it. "You're right about that. You found the publisher and his address."

"But not the author," Mrs. Farmstead said. "The book must never have been registered with the Copyright Office."

"But it had a copyright notice."

"That's the law. You can copyright it by putting on the notice, but you don't have to complete the registration. The author may not even have wanted it copyrighted. The publisher may have printed the notice automatically."

"So," Adrian said, "what do we do next?"

"We find the publisher and force him to reveal what he knows."

"The name and location of the author?"

Mrs. Farmstead nodded. "And that's what we're going to do. But I've got a question for you: if your suspicions are correct, what does it mean?"

"I don't even like to talk about it—it's too bizarre."

"Trust me. I've read a lot of bizarre scenarios while I was waiting for customers."

Adrian looked out the window past Mrs. Farmstead. Time had passed, and they were flying over the mountainous northern corner of New Mexico. "I've got a theory," he said, "that Winterbotham, or whoever he really is, was in a position to intercept a communication of extra-terrestrial origin."

"From aliens?"

Adrian nodded.

"What kind of communication?"

Adrian shrugged. "Radio. Gravity waves. DNA. Some kind of message, anyway. It may have had some general images or it may have consisted only of the designs. Or Winterbotham may have received or deciphered something that looked vaguely like a spaceship and the engines that powered it, and invented the rest. Only somebody—maybe the people he worked for—didn't want him to publish it in some normal fashion, and he had to sneak it out in a way that wouldn't be suspected."

"That's bizarre, all right."

They were silent for a long time, thinking about the bizarreness of their mission.

"The only thing that makes it seem at all plausible," Adrian said finally, "is where we found it."

"And your belief in it," Mrs. Farmstead said.

"There's that," Adrian agreed. "That most of all. Trained people recognize authenticity. There's something about all this that speaks to me."

"Like books and art," Mrs. Farmstead said. "Only sometimes even the authorities fail to recognize fakes."

Adrian nodded. "I didn't say it was infallible. Sometimes wish-fulfillment gets in the way. But there's more: the fact that there may be only one copy. The anonymity of the author. The denial of the publisher."

"The burning of the Book Nook."

"Even if we call that an accident," Adrian said. "My theory is that if the designs are real, aliens have sent us the means to reach the stars."

"Why would they do that, Adrian?"

"That's the question," Adrian said. "And there's no way to get the answer unless we build the spaceship and go visit the aliens. There may be people who don't want us to go. Or don't want the world to have the technology implied by those designs. And they're the ones we need to watch out for."

By that time they were preparing to land in Phoenix, and there was no more time for speculation.

————

Joel Simpson lived in a small town in northern Arizona. Adrian had rented a car in Phoenix. He and Mrs. Farmstead had argued about that and the need for Adrian to produce a driver's license, until Adrian had pointed out that his name had never been associated with the book or Mrs. Farmstead's store or her telephone inquiries. They had driven north on Highway 17, through deserts and national forests, past Indian reservations, through Flagstaff, and close by the Lowell Observatory where much of the world's apprehensions about aliens had started with Percival Lowell's observations of the "canals" on Mars and his speculations about intelligent Martians nourishing their dying planet. Adrian wanted to stop, but Mrs. Farmstead vetoed the idea.

"The fewer marks we leave along the trail, the more difficulty anyone will have trying to follow us," she said.

They came to a stop, toward evening, in a little town not far from the Grand Canyon. Mrs. Farmstead wanted to make a side trip to see the gorge carved out by the Colorado River over the ages. "I've always wanted to see it," she said. "I never thought I'd be this close, and I may not have another chance."

Adrian vetoed that notion. "We don't have time. Maybe in the morning." But he knew, and she knew, that if their mission was successful they would be leaving in a hurry.

Mrs. Farmstead looked at the town with what Adrian interpreted as dismay. There was a business section two blocks long, with a grocery store, an official building of some kind, two filling stations, one with a café attached, and several vacant storefronts. This was a town that was being emptied of its citizens like water evaporating from a desert pond. "In a town this size," she said, "strangers will stick out like weeds in a flower bed. And all we have for an address is a post-office box."

"We'll stop at one of the filling stations for gas and ask for a motel or a bed-and-breakfast," Adrian said. "Say we're going to head on over to the Grand Canyon in the morning."

Mrs. Farmstead looked at him with admiration. "Nothing like sticking close to the truth," she said.

They chose the nearest filling station. A talkative clerk told them about the best bed-and-breakfast this side of Flagstaff, run by his aunt Isabel and if they told her that Sylvester had sent them, she'd be sure to treat them right. "And give him a fee for touting the place," Mrs. Farmstead told Adrian later. Now she said to the clerk, "Isn't this the place where that fellow publishes those UFO books?"

The clerk looked blank.

"I've read some of them," Mrs. Farmstead said. "Simpson, I think his name is?"

"Never heard of him," the clerk said.

His aunt was more helpful. "Simpson? He must be the odd duck who believes in flying saucers. I've heard he had something to do with books. He lives the other side of town."

"How would we find it?" Adrian asked.

Mrs. Farmstead added quickly, "If we wanted to look him up, maybe say hello."

"I'd have to draw you a map," Isabel said. "No house numbers in a town like this."

Adrian looked from the map to Mrs. Farmstead. "Thanks," she said. "Maybe we'll drive past there on our way to the Canyon in the morning." She gave Adrian a nudge.

"We're sort of night-owls," he said. "Do you suppose we could have a key to the outside door in case we come in late?"

"A key?" Isabel said. "Nobody locks their doors around here."

Adrian looked at her with astonishment.

"How wonderful!" Mrs. Farmstead said. "Come on, dear." They had introduced themselves as mother and son, and now, being maternal and filial respectively, they linked arms and walked out into the narrow street, redolent with the smell of desert wind and cactus. Adrian half expected to see tumbleweeds rolling down the street.

Simpson's house, if that was what it was, was dark except for a single lighted window, perhaps a study or a bedroom or a living room. The night was black, but they could make out the outline of the building—it seemed square and low, perhaps adobe or imitation adobe. When the light went out, Mrs. Farmstead reached into her handbag and pulled out a flashlight.

"You are resourceful," Adrian said.

"A woman living alone has to be prepared for anything," Mrs. Farmstead said. She led the way to a detached garage.

"We're not looking for a car, Mrs. Farmstead," Adrian said.

"A small publisher can't afford to pay for storage," Mrs. Farmstead said, "and it makes sense to keep his records where he keeps his stock."

The side door to the garage was unlocked. Isabel had been right about doors. They entered quietly, and Mrs. Farmstead played her light around the inside. The only trace of an automobile was old oil stains on the concrete floor and a lingering odor of gasoline. But one wall was filled with books on rough shelves; sealed cardboard boxes were stacked against the back wall; on the near side were a gray metal desk, a telephone, a fax machine, and a gray metal filing cabinet.

Adrian inspected the books, and Mrs. Farmstead looked through the files in the cabinet, starting with the bottom drawer. "Simpson was right," Adrian whispered. "There's only two books: *The Aliens Are Here* and *UFOs and What They Mean.* No *Gift from the Stars.*"

"Means nothing," she said. "No Winterbotham file either, but then there wouldn't be, would there?" She riffled through the files in the other drawers. "It would take days to go through all these. I've always wondered about movies, how they can come up with the incriminating file in a few minutes."

"Wouldn't there have to be tax records?" Adrian asked.

"Ah!" she said and turned to look for files marked by the year. She chose the one for six years earlier. "Aha!" she said. "Publishing costs for *Gift from the Stars*, and payment of one hundred dollars to someone named—"

"Peter Cavendish," a voice said from the door.

They jerked and turned. A small man in a red-and-black plaid robe over blue pajamas stood in the doorway with a large shotgun in his hand. It was pointed at Mrs. Farmstead.

———

The garage was redolent with the electric scent of tension, but Mrs. Farmstead stared coolly. "You're very quick to reveal information you've been asked to forget!"

The barrel of the shotgun began to droop. "What do you mean?" the stranger asked.

"Maybe you'd also tell us where we could find Peter Cavendish?" Mrs. Farmstead continued.

The shotgun barrel lifted again. "Why would you ask that?"

"The people we work for would like to know how much you'd reveal to strangers."

"You mean you work for—?"

"What do you think? You know what you were told: To turn over all copies of the book and wipe out all evidence of its existence. Well, we've discovered that at least one copy of the book has survived, and people are making inquiries. And now we find, Mr. Joel Simpson, that a record of the author survives in your file."

The shotgun pointed to the stained floor. "I didn't know," Simpson said. He was thin and nervous. "I wish you people would make up your minds—the IRS says I gotta keep the information, you say I gotta get rid of it. What's a guy to do?"

"Bull!" Adrian said, entering the conversation for the first time. "The IRS doesn't care anymore. You just forgot."

"Just like you're going to forget Peter Cavendish," Mrs. Farmstead said. "And just to prove it you're going to tell us where he is."

Simpson's eyes got suspicious. "If you're one of them, you know where he is."

"Of course we know," Adrian said. "We just want to know if you know, so that when we tell you to forget it, you'll know what to forget."

Simpson turned that over in his mind without seeming to unravel it. "He's in a mental hospital in Topeka, Kansas," he said.

"That wasn't so hard, was it?" Mrs. Farmstead said. "Now forget it! Forget Peter Cavendish! And forget you ever saw us!"

"Yes, ma'am," Simpson said. "You bet. I never want to see any of you again. You're worse than aliens."

"What do you know about aliens?" Adrian asked sharply.

"Nothing!" Simpson said. "Nothing at all! I'm sorry I ever heard of them. I'll burn my books."

"Too much of a giveaway," Mrs. Farmstead said. "Keep everything as it was. Just forget the rest!"

"Yes, ma'am—and sir."

Outside, in the car, Adrian said. "Quick thinking back there."

"I read a scene like that in a spy novel," Mrs. Farmstead said. "Ian Fleming, maybe. I've read so many I get them mixed up. You were quick on the pick-up."

"Do you think he'll notify anyone?"

"Not for a while. Then maybe the shock will wear off and he'll begin to think about it, maybe wonder why we were sneaking around in the middle of the night, maybe analyze your nonsense about revealing Cavendish's whereabouts so that he would know what to forget."

"It was all I could think of at the time," Adrian said.

"Don't apologize for anything that works."

"Maybe he doesn't have a contact."

"Not likely," Mrs. Farmstead said. "They always leave a number to call in case people start making inquiries or start nosing around. Sooner or later he'll think to check."

"So sooner rather than later we'd better get out of here," Adrian said.

When they got back to the bed-and-breakfast, Isabel wasn't around. She was in her room asleep, they hoped. They messed up their beds to look slept-in, Adrian left money for the night's stay on the end table in the entry hall along with a note Mrs. Farmstead had written saying "Decided to make an early start for the Canyon. Here's money for the rooms. Thanks for everything," and they tiptoed out, easing the door shut behind them.

They headed back to Flagstaff, bypassing the Grand Canyon and the Lowell Observatory once more, before turning east on Highway 40. Mrs. Farmstead dozed in the passenger seat until the sun came up just before they reached Gallup.

"A mental hospital, Adrian?" she said. "I think I was dreaming about mental hospitals and a patient named Cavendish."

"I've been thinking about that, too. But it figures, doesn't it? Where's a better place to stash Cavendish? Where he can talk all he likes about aliens and messages from outer space and spaceships."

"We've got to figure out a plan of action," Mrs. Farmstead said, "and how we're going to protect ourselves."

By the time they arrived in Albuquerque their plans were complete, and all they had to do was check in the car and catch the first flight to Kansas City. Adrian used their own names again, trying not to glance around the pueblo-style airport to see whether someone was watching. "In movies," Mrs. Farmstead said, "people always give themselves away by acting as if someone were watching them. Almost as if they expect to be nabbed, and, of course, they are."

"By now, of course," Adrian said, "they may have traced the license plate on the rental car and have my name. They could be here in a few hours, maybe, but surely not before we've left. I wish we'd thought to make up fake IDs."

"In novels," Mrs. Farmstead said, "pursuers never get thrown off the scent. They'll be waiting for us in Topeka."

"Life isn't a novel," Adrian said. "In a book people get caught because the plot gets more complicated if they're caught, and if the pursuers were thrown off, that would be the end of a story, wouldn't it?"

Mrs. Farmstead nodded. "But it helps to anticipate the worst scenario. That way we won't be surprised."

"We'll have our insurance," Adrian said.

At that moment their flight was called and they passed through the metal detectors and onto the plane, not looking back.

————

Topeka had three major mental hospitals, the Veterans Administration, the state, and the Menninger Foundation. The first two had developed mostly because of the psychiatrists and reputation accumulating around Will Menninger's pioneering work. They weren't far apart, but Adrian thought random inquiries would only tip off pursuers. Maybe he and Mrs. Farmstead could think of a way to narrow the search.

"He probably wouldn't be a veteran," Adrian said.

"But a government agency might be able to put him away there," Mrs. Farmstead said. "Maybe manufacture documents? Pull strings?"

"Possibly," Adrian conceded. They were sitting in another rented car in a large shopping center, having already spent some time in a computer service center. On this occasion, Mrs. Farmstead had signed for the car in Kansas City, leaving a different trail to slow potential pursuers. "But government red tape might make it nearly impossible to contact a patient, at least in the time we have."

"Before they catch up with us."

"Or intercept us. As for the state hospital—I don't know the rules in this state, but wouldn't he have to be a resident before he could be admitted?"

"You'd think so," Mrs. Farmstead said. "That leaves—"

"The Menninger Clinic." He glanced into the rearview mirror and then back at Mrs. Farmstead. "Do you ever feel like we may be fleeing from phantoms?"

Mrs. Farmstead nodded. "The guilty flee," she said. "But the worst-case scenario—"

"I'm tired of subterfuge," Adrian said. "Let's play it straight."

Ten minutes found them on the campus of the Menninger Clinic. It was an attractive place, not like a hospital or institution at all, with trees and lawns and garden beds and buildings scattered here and there, and the breezes and green odors of a park. In the middle of everything was an office building. After five minutes of winding roads, and half an hour of questioning by security guards, they finally reached a reception desk.

"We're looking for a patient named Peter Cavendish," Adrian said. "We've been told he was hospitalized in Topeka, and we thought he might be here."

"Are you relatives?" the pleasant young woman asked.

Adrian shook his head. "We came across a fascinating book he wrote, and we thought we'd take the chance we might be able to meet him while we were passing through."

"A book?" She turned to her computer and clicked a few keys. "Yes, we have a Peter Cavendish, but you need a written request in advance that must be processed by the resident's treatment team."

Adrian and Mrs. Farmstead exchanged glances.

"Golly," Mrs. Farmstead said, "we're only going to be in Topeka a few hours."

"It might help Mr. Cavendish to talk to someone who has read his book," Adrian added.

"And admired it," Mrs. Farmstead said.

The receptionist hesitated. "Let me call his attending psychiatrist, Dr. Freeman." She turned to her telephone and soon began talking to someone. She swung back to Adrian and Mrs. Farmstead. "What's the name of the book?"

Adrian hesitated and said, "*Gift from the Stars.*"

The receptionist gave the title into the telephone and listened while Adrian's breath caught in his chest. "Okay," she said, "I'll get an orderly to take you to the unit."

The building looked like a two-story brick apartment building. Inside, it was like an attractively laid-out and furnished home. They waited in an off-white "day room" with a cream-colored sofa and brown, tapestry-covered easy chairs, framed landscapes on the wall, and a television set in one corner, while the orderly disappeared down a hallway. He returned in a minute or two with a medium-sized man in a dark shirt and slacks and a cheerful Scandinavian sweater; it was white with red reindeer. The newcomer had his hands in his pockets. He seemed to be middle-aged, perhaps in his fifties, with blond hair and blue eyes and a calm expression. Adrian wouldn't have given him a second glance on the street unless he had looked closer and noticed the stiff, almost apprehensive set of the man's shoulders and the way his eyes kept scanning the room but never looked directly at Adrian or Mrs. Farmstead.

"Peter Cavendish?" Adrian said.

The man nodded.

"I'll be in the next room if you need me," the orderly said.

Cavendish looked after the orderly until he was clearly out of earshot and said, "Are you from *them*?"

"Them?"

Cavendish's glance flicked back and forth. "You know. *Them.*"

"No," Adrian said. "We just came to see you. We read your book, *Gift from the Stars*. We wanted to talk to you about it."

"*They* don't want me to talk about it."

"They're not here. You can talk to us."

"How do I know it's not a trick?"

"Do we look like tricky people?" Mrs. Farmstead said. She leaned forward, her hands spread open as if to show that she was concealing nothing. "I sell books. He designs airplanes."

"And spaceships," Adrian said.

Cavendish looked at them for the first time, and his face relaxed, as if he had been wearing a mask and the fasteners had broken. Adrian realized that Cavendish had been holding himself together. Tears appeared on the lower lids of his eyes. "You've come to rescue me," he said.

"The orderly said you could walk away any time," Adrian said.

"That's what they tell you," Cavendish said darkly.

"But we have come to rescue your ideas," Mrs. Farmstead said. "Could you tell us about the book?"

"It's all true," Cavendish said.

Adrian nodded. "We believe it. But what part—"

"Everything. The aliens are here. You may be aliens for all I know." Cavendish's body tensed again.

"We're just people," Mrs. Farmstead said. "Like you."

"That's what they'd say, wouldn't they?"

"I'm interested in the spaceship designs," Adrian said. "I'm an aerospace engineer, and I think I could build a spaceship from those designs."

"Yes," Cavendish said. "I got them out of there, you know."

"From the NASA project?" Adrian guessed.

Cavendish looked puzzled. "From SETI, of course. Cosmic rays. Energetic stuff. Too energetic to be natural, the physicists told me. Figure it out, it makes a picture. Right? You've got to decipher the code. But they make it easy. They want you to figure it out."

"Anti-cryptography," Adrian said.

"But then you don't know," Cavendish said. He looked bewildered.

"Do they want you to come? Why don't they come here instead? Why don't the others want the information to get out? What will happen to the world if everyone knows?" He was getting agitated. "Why did they tell us? Why do they want us to come? Do they want to torture us? Dissect us? Make us slaves? Eat us?" Tears began trickling down his face.

"It's all right, Mr. Cavendish," Adrian said. He felt like backing away from the man standing in front of him, looking almost normal but acting strangely.

Mrs. Farmstead had better instincts. She moved forward and put her arm around Cavendish's shoulder and led him to the sofa. She sat down beside him and held his hand.

"Are there any other drawings?" Adrian asked.

"They destroyed them," Cavendish said more quietly. "The other aliens. The ones who are here. The ones who don't want us to go." He glanced around slyly. "But I hid the real ones." He looked apprehensive again. "Maybe they're right, though. Maybe it was all a mistake."

A change in the light and a puff of breeze alerted them more than the muffled sound of the door opening behind them. "I think you've talked long enough, Peter," a calm voice said.

———

Cavendish jumped up nervously as Adrian and Mrs. Farmstead turned toward the door. A tall, sandy-haired man in a tweed jacket and imitation horn-rimmed glasses stood framed in the doorway. He looked a bit like Cary Grant but sounded more like Clint Eastwood.

"Fred," he said, and they turned to see the orderly in the entrance to the hall, "I think Peter has had enough company for one day. Take him back to his room and give him a Xanax."

"Yes, Dr. Freeman," the orderly said. He took Cavendish's arm and they disappeared down the hallway. Cavendish gave a single anguished look back at them before he returned to his unnatural calm.

"So," Adrian said, turning to the psychiatrist, "you're Cavendish's physician?"

Freeman nodded. "And who are you?"

"My name is Adrian Mast. And this is Mrs. Farmstead."

"Frances Farmstead," she said.

"We were hoping to get some information from Cavendish about a book he published half a dozen years ago," Adrian said.

"The famous book," Freeman said.

"What's famous about it?" Adrian asked. "As far as I know there's only copy, and we've got it."

"Peter talks about it a lot," Freeman said. "Maybe we'd better sit. We may have more than a little to talk about." He walked into the room and sat down in one of the easy chairs, and motioned Adrian and Mrs. Farmstead to the facing sofa. "You're not casual visitors as you suggested to the receptionist."

Adrian and Mrs. Farmstead looked at each other. Adrian said, "Not casual—in the sense that we weren't just passing through. We sought Cavendish out. But casual in the sense that we represent nobody but ourselves and our curiosity."

"Curiosity about *Gift from the Stars*?"

Adrian nodded. "Do you believe in the book, Dr. Freeman?"

"I've never seen a copy."

Adrian looked at Mrs. Farmstead. She unzipped her large purse, rummaged around in the central pocket, pulled out the book, and handed it to Adrian who passed it on to Freeman. The psychiatrist turned it over in his hands and then opened the cover to the title page and to page one. "Now I believe in it," he said and held up a hand, "though not in the sense you mean. But, more to the point, you believe in it."

Adrian cleared his throat nervously. "At this point I have the urge to convince you that we're not crazy. We're not UFO believers. We don't think aliens are zooming around, abducting people, maybe even passing for humans. But could some of the book be derived from reality rather than imagination?"

"Anything is possible, Mr. Mast," Freeman said carefully. "You can find truth in some unlikely places and, as the French say, even a stopped clock is right twice a day. But this is the sort of book I'd expect a paranoid schizophrenic to write, if one wrote a book. Not many of them do; they don't have the attention span. But Peter wrote this book before he came to us."

"And how did he come to you?" Mrs. Farmstead asked. "Was he more disturbed then? Did he have any explanation for his condition?"

"Those are not the kind of questions I feel free to answer. Speaking as his physician." Freeman put his hands together. "You're the ones who need to justify your presence here."

"Turn to the appendices," Adrian said. He waited while Freeman leafed to the back of the book. "Those are spaceship designs. I'm an aerospace engineer, and I would stake my reputation on the fact that those designs are genuine. I could build a spaceship from these if I could find something more detailed. And if I could develop the technology they imply."

Freeman nodded slowly. "I'll take your word for it. Not that I believe it. I have no proof, you see."

"Any more than you have proof of Cavendish's—condition," Adrian said. He almost said "insanity" before he realized that psychiatrists probably found that word offensive.

"Could it have been induced?" Mrs. Farmstead said. "Is Cavendish on drugs? Was he placed here?"

Freeman shook his head. "He is on drugs, of course. He needs to be calmed occasionally, as you saw just now, and we're trying to restore his sense of reality by restoring his chemical balances. But paranoid schizophrenia is a genetic predisposition sometimes triggered by an emotional crisis."

"Not by drugs?" Adrian said.

Freeman chose his words carefully. "He came here talking about aliens and conspiracies, referred to us from a hospital in California. This is a place less conducive to theories of persecution. It was thought he had a better chance of recovery."

"And what if we told you that there may be evidence of a conspiracy to suppress the distribution of this book?" Adrian said. "Maybe Cavendish isn't crazy." There, he had used a word even more likely to offend.

Freeman didn't seem offended. "He suffers from schizophrenia. You can take my word for that. And for the fact that I'm not a member of any conspiracy. I am trying to cure his condition, not cause it." Freeman stood up. "I think you're reading far more into this than is there. Peter Cavendish was a member of a team searching for signs of extraterrestrial intelligence. He had the background and ability to draw these designs, even make them plausible, perhaps even workable. But, like you, he surrendered to his desire that what he wanted to be true was really true. To oversimplify, the conflict created in him by this self-deception, and the necessary supporting details of a conspiracy to keep him from going public, triggered a psychotic reaction that brought him here. When he is able to recognize that, he will be on the road to recovery."

"You mean," Mrs. Farmstead said, "when he's willing to accept your version of reality."

"The world's version," Freeman said.

Adrian and Mrs. Farmstead stood up. Adrian shook his head as if trying to avoid the inevitable. "I hope," he said, "you won't find it necessary to report this incident."

"There is nobody to report it to," Freeman said, "except the team that supervises Peter's case. I have to note your visit, but if I can I won't elaborate on your beliefs. In return I'll need something from you: by your support for Peter's delusions, you have given his treatment a setback, and I would like your promise that you won't disturb him again."

Adrian and Mrs. Farmstead nodded.

"Goodbye, Mrs. Farmstead," Freeman said. "Mr. Mast. Give up this notion. You're only wasting your time."

"Goodbye, Dr. Freeman," Adrian said, "and thanks for your consideration." He reached out his hand. Freeman looked at it for a moment and then, with a start, returned the copy of *Gift from the Stars*.

———

Adrian sat disconsolately at the counter in the coffee shop, a cup of black coffee cooling unnoticed in front of him. "So Cavendish is crazy, and so are we for chasing after something as weird as this."

"You're taking Dr. Freeman's word for it?" Mrs. Farmstead asked.

"Aren't you?"

"Well, maybe. Freeman could be working for the people who stopped Cavendish's publication, who wanted him hospitalized. But he seems genuine." A wicked smile creased her face. "But just because a person is crazy doesn't mean he doesn't have a few sane thoughts. Like Dr. Freeman said about the stopped clock."

Hope flickered in Adrian's eyes. "That's right."

Mrs. Farmstead took a sip of her hot tea. "Dr. Freeman suggested that maybe the stress of writing the book, of inventing what he wanted to be true, set him off. But what if it wasn't that—what if it was the predicament of knowing he had stumbled onto some fantastic truth and then it was suppressed?"

"And of not knowing the right thing to do," Adrian picked up excitedly. "Maybe, he thought, the people who wanted to destroy the information were right. Why were the aliens sending the plans? What did they want from us? Why did they want us to have a spaceship that could reach the stars? Why didn't they simply hop in their spaceships and come to visit us?"

"Exactly," Mrs. Farmstead said. "Those aren't easy questions. They might make anyone flip out. That's what Cavendish kept trying to say."

"I'll admit," Adrian said, "questions about the aliens and their motives have run through my mind, too, while I'm trying to go to sleep and sometimes when I wake up during the night."

"And like the bumper sticker when I was young," Mrs. Farmstead said, "'just because you're paranoid doesn't mean people aren't after you.'"

"But if that were the case," Adrian said, depression edging back, "you'd think that somebody would be tapping us on the shoulder about now."

"Mr. Mast, Mrs. Farmstead," a voice said behind them. "That sounds like a cue."

They turned. Behind them was the orderly named Fred. He had been wearing white pants and a white jacket at the Clinic, but now he had changed into a rumpled brown jacket over his white pants, and he looked like a bookish graduate student.

"You?" Adrian said.

Fred nodded. "You know how much orderlies make? They paid me pretty good just to keep my eyes open and let them know if anybody came around asking about Mr. Cavendish. Look, there's somebody who wants to talk to you."

"Suppose we don't want to talk to him?" Mrs. Farmstead said.

Fred shrugged. "Up to you. But sooner or later you're going to talk to him, and the sooner it is the sooner you can stop looking over your shoulder."

"Are you threatening us?" Adrian asked.

Fred spread his hands. "You see any threats? You know, working around a mental institution you get some insights into behavior. I've learned this much: it's better to face the unknown than to run from it."

"And where do we do this?" Adrian asked.

"Is this where some goons throw us in a black limousine and whisk us off to Washington?" Mrs. Farmstead said.

"You been watching too many thrillers," Fred said. "You can go wherever you want, or you can follow me to Forbes Field, where a man has just arrived in an Air Force jet. He's waiting for you."

Adrian looked at Mrs. Farmstead, and Mrs. Farmstead looked at Adrian. Adrian shrugged. "Let's get it over with," he said.

By the time they reached Forbes Field, the sun was setting. It had been a long day that had started far from this spot, and there had been little sleep and less food. They were tired and hungry.

Waiting at the back of an unused hangar at the airfield was a fat man sitting at a folding table. Mrs. Farmstead nudged Adrian and said, out of the corner of her mouth, "Sydney Greenstreet." The fat man didn't laugh like Greenstreet, however, from the gut, his belly shaking. He didn't laugh at all. Sitting behind a portable table, he scowled at Adrian and Mrs. Farmstead as if assessing what kind of punishment he could mete out to the civilians who had made him travel all this distance and put up with such discomfort. It *was* discomfort. He overflowed the metal chair he sat on, gingerly, as if it were about to collapse beneath him.

"Well," Adrian said, "then it's all true."

"Truth depends on where you stand," the fat man said.

"Or sit," Adrian said, looking around for other chairs. There were none in that vast expanse of empty hangar. Greenstreet was going to make them stand in front of him like convicts awaiting judgment. "Let's have some truth, then. I'm Adrian Mast, and this is Frances Farmstead, and we've been looking for Peter Cavendish and the alien plans for building a spaceship. Now, who are you and why have you asked us here?"

The fat man was wearing a dark suit. It had a matching vest; nobody wore vests anymore, but his had a purpose. He reached into a vest pocket, retrieved a calling card with two fingers, and flicked it onto the table in front of Adrian. Adrian picked it up and looked at it. It read: "William Makepeace." And under that: "Consultant."

"William Makepeace," Mrs. Farmstead said. "Wasn't that Thackeray's name?"

"My parents were great readers," Makepeace said.

"And what gives you the authority to summon us here?" Adrian asked.

"I'm in charge of the Cavendish affair," Makepeace said.

"It's an affair, then," Mrs. Farmstead said, "like an Agatha Christie mystery."

"An affair," Makepeace said, "is something less than a case and something more than a situation."

"Hah!" Adrian said.

"Let us be reasonable," Makepeace said. "You are idealists; I am a pragmatist. You deal in dreams; I deal in what is. One of us has to convince the other."

"You first," Adrian said. "Are the spaceship designs authentic?"

"As far as I know," Makepeace said. "But I'm no expert in alien communications, nor in deciphering codes, nor in spaceship design. I've been told by those who ought to know that they seem genuine."

"And will they work?"

Makepeace shrugged. It was like a tide of jello under his coat. "We haven't gone that far."

"Why not?"

"That part was unimportant."

"My god! What was important?"

"You want to go to the stars," Makepeace said. "I see that. Sensible people, of whom I am one, want to see that we don't destroy each other. We don't care if you go to the stars, Mr. Mast, as long as we can survive in some approximation of civilization."

"What in the name of everything holy does that have to do with building a spaceship?"

"Nothing," Makepeace said, "but our experts point out that the antimatter collectors—" He stopped as Adrian jumped. "Yes, they are designs for antimatter collectors, according to people who ought to know. If we built them, Mr. Mast, what do you think would happen?"

"Besides getting us to the stars," Mrs. Farmstead said.

"Quite right," Makepeace said. "Besides that."

"I suppose they would lead to the development of new energy systems, maybe generation in orbit," Adrian said.

"You are quick, Mr. Mast. No wonder you caught on to the designs in *Gift from the Stars*. But what comes after energy generation in orbit?"

Now it was Adrian's turn to shrug. "I give up. What?"

"Cheap energy, for one thing," Makepeace said. "Our experts predict that we could beam down energy from orbit at a fraction of the cost of current sources."

"What's wrong with that?" Adrian asked.

"What do you think will happen when entire industries get displaced, virtually overnight?"

"It's happened before," Adrian said.

"But not so quickly, and not in a way that will transform the balance of power. Do you think that the energy-producing nations won't fight, maybe resort to financial strategies that would upset the world's economy, or terrorism, or even war?"

Adrian shook his head. "Buy them off. Buy them up. Cut them in. Give them free energy. Give them a share of the process. Anyway, oil and gas are far more valuable as biological raw materials than as fuel."

"Ah, Mr. Mast, that requires forethought and rational decision-making, and the nations of the world aren't good at those things."

"Maybe they could see that cheap, inexhaustible energy makes everything possible," Mrs. Farmstead said, "from feeding the hungry and housing the homeless to raising their standards of living to the level of the western nations without destroying the world's resources, without pollution. We could clean up the environment. We could do anything."

"Cheap energy could make a heaven on Earth," Adrian said. "It could solve all our problems."

"Mr. Mast, Mrs. Farmstead," Makepeace said pityingly, "that will never happen. People aren't willing to give up their little disputes, their ancient hatreds, their petty jealousies. And, you see, antimatter makes one other thing possible."

"What?"

"Bigger and better bombs. Big enough to shatter this planet, I'm told. Do you have an answer for that?"

Adrian looked down. "No," he said. "You just have to have faith that people are better than that, that they will see the promise and hold off on the destruction. That's your job, you and the people you work for, to convince them."

"I haven't convinced you."

"We're on the side of the angels," Mrs. Farmstead said. "Or the aliens."

Makepeace spread his arms out, palms up, as if helpless in the face of irresistible facts. "But we can't take the chance. Sure, we could have a lot more of everything or we could end up with nothing at all. In that scheme of things, the status quo wins every time. So, you see, you have a choice. Either you give up this foolishness or—"

"Or what?" Adrian said fiercely.

"Or we will have to discredit you," Makepeace said. "We can do that, you know. The resources of the government are massive; they can be mobilized to make you part of the UFO fringe cultists. You will be destroyed, along with that book you have in your possession and whatever copies you may have made."

Adrian shook his head. "I don't think so."

"What do you mean, Mr. Mast?" Makepeace said. "I hope you haven't done something foolish."

"Depends on what you mean by 'foolish,'" Mrs. Farmstead said. "You know those old movies where the hero leaves the information in the hands of his lawyer, in case he gets killed, or in a safe-deposit box?"

"Ridiculous," Makepeace said.

"That's what we thought," Mrs. Farmstead said. "They're always killing the lawyer or looting the safe-deposit box, or the newspaper editor is part of the conspiracy. So we put everything on the Internet this morning."

"Bah!" Makepeace's relief was clear. "The Internet is filled with junk nobody believes."

"We know," Adrian said. "So we labeled the statement as a NASA news release—we didn't know then that it was SETI. But first we inserted the designs into NASA's database."

For the first time Makepeace looked uncertain. "You can't do that!" He shivered as he considered Adrian's confidence. "They can be found, erased."

"By now they're all around the world. People must be accessing the database already."

"The designs can be discredited, ridiculed."

"Scientists and engineers will recognize their validity just as I did.

Particularly scientists and engineers in other countries. You'll never know who might be taking the designs seriously. As in the race for the atom bomb, the U.S. can't afford to come in second."

"The genie is out of the bottle, Mr. Makepeace," Mrs. Farmstead said. "I think you'd better make your three wishes."

"You poor, stupid people!" Makepeace said. "You don't know what you've done!"

"We've just given humanity the stars," Adrian said. "It's your job to see that humanity doesn't destroy itself first."

"And how do you propose we do that?"

"I suggest you mobilize all those resources you were talking about, get them behind the release of the designs, take credit for it, swing public opinion into the realization that this is a legitimate gift from beneficent aliens, and we have been given the chance to make everybody rich and happy."

"And let some of us go to the stars," Mrs. Farmstead said.

"Oh my god!" Makepeace said and put his face down into his hands. Then, slowly, he pulled himself to his feet and plodded toward the hangar exit like a man who had just realized that he was old and fat and would never feel any better than he did now.

Adrian looked at Mrs. Farmstead. "Well, Frances," he said. He held out his arm and she took it. "I hope I may call you Frances."

"Any time, Adrian."

"What we opened may be the genie's bottle, or it may be Pandora's box," Adrian said. "Whichever it is, we're going to live in interesting times."

"If it's the genie's bottle, let's be sure we make the right wishes," Mrs. Farmstead said. "If it's Pandora's box, we must remind ourselves to be patient."

And they walked out of the hangar into a night in which the stars seemed close enough to touch.

I sell what all men desire.

MATTHEW BOULTON

⊨

Part Two

POW'R

THE OBJECTS WERE BLACK AGAINST the overwhelming brilliance of the sun. Hovering just outside the coronasphere like moths drawn to a flame, their wings seeming to flutter in the solar wind, they maintained their positions and their existence against the elemental forces acting upon them. If they had been alive, they would have been unbelievable evidence of the variety of existence, but they were even more remarkable: they were machines built from alien specifications to liberate humanity from the Solar System in which it had been imprisoned. They were a gift from the stars.

Frances Farmstead replayed the tape, but this time she let it continue until the end, when a shape like a transparent shark drifted across the screen. The sun shone through the image almost undiminished, and the black moths could still be distinguished if she peered, but something halfway between an after-image and a sketch crossed in front of the sun and the mechanical creatures sucking its energy. It was a ship—or the Platonic idea of a ship—where no ship existed, like a reminder of a promise unfulfilled, like someone walking across her grave.

Frances looked around the shop as if comparing it with a bookstore she once had owned. But this was spacious where the Book Nook had been narrow and quiet, and the books that had stood at attention upon shelves and stared at the ceiling from tables had been replaced by the backs of videotapes and the jewel-boxes of CD-ROM disks. Between the shelves were classic movie posters framed in white: *The Day the Earth Stood Still*, *The Thing*, *The War of the Worlds*, *Attack of the Flying Saucers*, *Independence Day*, *Contact*, and *Star Wars: The Final Victory*.

Frances had outlived her husband and her son, and her daughter had stopped communicating after Frances had opted for rejuvenation, and now Frances had outlived the age of reading.

She sighed, as if coming to a decision, and spoke to her computer. "Phone Adrian Mast," she said. She could hear the connection click and then the telephone begin to ring, but the screen remained blank. After three rings, the sound stopped and a computerized voice announced, "This number is no longer in service. For directory assistance consult your local website."

"Directory assistance," she told the computer. After a few moments the computer said, "Directory assistance has no listing for Adrian Mast."

"Locate Adrian Mast using all available databases," she said. She tried to suppress a feeling of alarm. The minutes passed slowly.

Finally the computer spoke. "I have identified eleven Adrian Masts, but none is the person you seek. As far as my resources can determine, that person does not exist and has never existed."

Typical computer literalness: how could a person have never existed if the computer had parameters to match? But that misplaced irritation was only Frances' effort to avoid panic. With Adrian she had hunted down the author of a UFO cult book in which Adrian had found what looked like, to him, working designs for an alien spaceship. Now Adrian had been eliminated from all the world's records.

It was like an Alfred Hitchcock movie. Why should Adrian disappear? Someone had gone to a great deal of effort to delete all traces of him. As if Adrian were—what? The man who knew too much?

Frances looked up at the posters on the far wall and then back at the computer. She idly tapped a few keys and then deleted the gibberish that appeared on the screen. Once people had reasons to get rid of Adrian.

But that was ten years ago, and nothing had happened since. Well, a great deal had happened to the world, but nothing had happened to Frances and Adrian except that they had drifted apart, once their adventure had ended. The alien technology had worked; devices were orbiting the sun. Solar moths were transforming the sun's energy into high-energy gamma rays and beaming them back to receivers in orbit where they were converted into antimatter. The entire process was marvelous beyond understanding, but seeing was believing, like the creation of an electric current when one rotates a wire through a magnetic field, or the illumination of an incandescent filament when a switch is turned. The documentary recently on her screen had mentioned "magic crystals" constructed of "strange matter," and the only thing that made it credible was that aliens had sent the plans and human scientists had blinked and then said it was possible. Power was available almost everywhere for almost nothing because in space the antimatter was combined with matter to create energy that was beamed to receivers on Earth that rebroadcast it around the world. . . .

That was all accomplished now, faster than anyone had thought possible, and everybody was rich and happy. The world was a different place. Space travel had been pushed aside, to be sure, but that was no reason for Adrian's disappearance. He was only a small voice unheard against a general background of self-satisfaction.

Only—if this were a Hitchcock movie, something else should be happening about now.

As if that were a cue, the door swung open, and a man and a woman in one-piece gray suits, like ill-matched twins, were inside the shop, not so much entering as materializing. They displayed no weapons, but their hands alone looked lethal. "You'll come with us," the woman said as if there were no question of non-compliance.

———

The man seated behind the ancient metal desk was tall and thin to the point of emaciation. His dark eyes seemed too large for his face. Frances thought of the movie *Freaks*, but in real life people couldn't stare unless they had paid admission. She looked away uncomfortably and studied the room; life was like a movie set—a person could tell a great deal about a character from his surroundings and even anticipate the actions that were going to happen. But this place offered few clues. It was a second-floor office in a twenty-five-story building in what had once been a thriving suburban business development. As the suburbs had sprawled farther into the countryside, they had dragged the administrative centers with them, but now the virtual office had replaced the old vertical units with their requirements for transportation and elevators and air-handling equipment and toilets and food and drink.

The office to which Frances had been escorted by the improbable twins matched its location. Its windows looked out upon buildings being razed and land returned to meadow and park. A shabby sofa covered in something that looked like green leather stood against one wall, and

equally shabby side chairs occupied each end of a battered wooden coffee table. Above the sofa was a tattered poster of a bullfight in Mexico
City. On the opposite wall was a reproduction of Van Gogh's *Sunflow-
ers*.

"Well, Mrs. Farmstead," a voice said from behind the desk, "are you
pleased with what you've done?" The voice was strangely familiar.

Frances looked back quickly. "Makepeace?"

The skeletal man nodded.

"What have they done to you?" The last time Frances had seen William Makepeace he had been an immense fat man, like Sydney Greenstreet in *The Maltese Falcon*, in a vast, empty hangar.

"The same thing they did to you," Makepeace said. "Or we did to
ourselves. We shed our weight with biogenetic help. With me the pen-
dulum swung a bit too far; on you it looks good, and the rejuvenation
process seems to have served you well."

"I cut my hair," Frances said absently, touching her gray bob. "But
what are you doing here? The national government is virtually out of
business."

Makepeace looked down at his bony hands. "A good bureaucrat can
always find work. A good bureaucrat is someone who does his job ef-
ficiently and quietly, accepts blame for whatever fails, and passes along
any credit to his superiors. Now I serve the Energy Board."

Nobody paid attention to the administration of utilities as long as
whatever they supplied was cheap and uninterrupted. But Frances had
heard of the Energy Board. She remembered vaguely that it was gov-
erned by five Chairs, each representing his or her continent and over-
seeing its distribution of the energy stolen from the sun.

"You asked me if I was pleased with what we had done, Adrian and
I, and I presume you mean the world we created when we released the
alien designs. And my answer is that the world has managed to absorb
alien technology without a tremor."

"Proving that you were right and the rest of us were wrong," Makepeace said.

"So it would seem. Has the world ever been in better shape? Energy
is being broadcast from mountain-top receiving stations, global warming is being reversed, pollution is being cleaned up, and the quality
of life around the world is being raised to Western standards. People
everywhere are happy and prosperous, education is universal, the arts
are flourishing, the ghettos are being depopulated and demolished, the
birthrate has dropped to a supportable level—what's not to like?"

"A virtual paradise," Makepeace said, as if in agreement.

Frances looked at Makepeace. "Virtual? Maybe that's the right word: utopia may not be here yet, but it isn't unimaginable. The only thing on which we haven't made any progress is spaceflight. No matter what we do, nobody will let us build a ship."

"You can't expect people to get excited about space when they have everything they need here on Earth," Makepeace said.

"That's one of the problems with paradise, isn't it?" Frances observed. "No one wants to leave."

The ceiling lights above them went dark. Frances twitched, but Makepeace sat unmoved, as if the occurrence were commonplace. The only light came through the windows behind him.

"If it's paradise," Makepeace said, "why are violent crimes and acts of terrorism on the increase?"

"That's news to me."

"And to most people. In good times bad news seems to drop below the horizon. Nobody notices."

The overhead lights came on again.

"Or maybe it doesn't get reported," Frances said.

"Censorship, Mrs. Farmstead?" Makepeace said. When he shook his head, it looked as if it might fall off his pipe-stem neck. "No need, and no means. The Energy Board is in the business of distributing energy, and it has no facilities for controlling the media. And even if it could, so much is available on the Internet that omissions in the media would be obvious. The answer is that nobody is paying attention."

"Except you."

Makepeace nodded carefully. "A few bureaucrats like me are paid to keep track and to ask why these things are happening."

"You didn't bring me here to get my opinion," Frances said flatly.

"Adrian Mast has disappeared," Makepeace said.

"So I found out. And there is no proof he ever existed."

"No electronic proof," Makepeace said.

"What do you mean?"

"It's not easy to delete physical evidence, written documents, files, that sort of thing," Makepeace said. "No one can work magic. But we've become dependent on electronic information, and a search program with instructions to eliminate anything it finds can remove the most available evidence of a life. But why would anyone do that?"

"I thought it was you," Frances said. She made a sweeping gesture that included the office and the bureaucracy it represented.

Makepeace shook his head. "Maybe it was Adrian himself."

Now it was Frances' turn to look skeptical.

"Aliens?" Makepeace suggested.

"That doesn't make sense," Frances said. "Why would they send us plans if they were here already?"

"To throw us off the track?"

"I still think it was you," Frances said, "or someone who looks a lot like you, or like you used to look. But whoever it was, I'm going to find out."

Makepeace looked as pleased as his death-mask face could manage. "I hoped you would, Mrs. Farmstead," he said.

———

Frances studied the cabin nestled in a grove of oak trees. A lot had happened to her and to Adrian in ten years, as well as to the rest of the world. Consultants seldom needed to meet in person with their clients anymore, and Adrian had retreated from his urban apartment to this rustic isolation. Frances had visited his apartment a couple of times, but Adrian's move had been part of the distancing process that had resulted, over the past half dozen years, in little more than holiday greetings. She hadn't even known he had moved until she had inquired for him at his former building.

Now she wondered whether she had identified the situation correctly. Maybe it wasn't a Hitchcock scenario after all; maybe it was a horror story or a mystery. It was important to get the genre right. Otherwise you wouldn't know what to look for or how to behave.

The cabin had no close neighbors. The taxi that had brought her had passed a few farmhouses along the way, but none were near enough for its occupants to keep track of Adrian's coming and goings. Here, far from the city, Frances missed its busybodies. In the police shows, neighbors witnessed whatever happened at any time of day or night; the difficulty was persuading them to talk. Maybe that was what Adrian had been looking for: anonymity. The only community that mattered to him was scattered around the world, and had only a faint hope of coming together, some day, out among the stars.

Finally, after circling the house and finding only a browsing rabbit to startle into leg-kicking terror and a quail that exploded from some underbrush, Frances decided to go in. The door was unlocked. In the movies an unlocked door was a cue for the detective to draw his pistol and sidle cautiously into the room beyond, steadying his weapon with both hands, aiming first one way and then the other. But she had no weapon, and she swung the door open and walked in, uncertainty fluttering in her stomach.

The doorway opened directly into a living room. It had smooth painted walls, casement windows, and a hardwood floor—not at all like the
inside of a cabin; it was one thing to desire the rough-hewn honesty
of a cabin and another to live in one. The only concession to tradition
was a big fireplace set into the left wall; in front of it was a rag rug and
a sofa upholstered in multi-colored tapestry, with matching chairs at
each end. A desk, with a closed laptop computer on top, stood against
the opposite wall. Beside the desk, a lawyer's bookcase with glass fronts
held three shelves of eclectic books. No one else was in the room, and
everything was neat, the way Frances remembered Adrian's apartment,
as if the cabin had been untenanted since he left or was taken.

Two doorways, one with a closed door, occupied the far wall. She
opened the door to the one on the left. Beyond was a bedroom with
an adjoining bath. The bed was made and the bedroom was empty and
neat; so was the bath, with folded towels draped in racks. The shower
was dry. The other doorway led to a kitchen and breakfast table with
four chairs. For the first time Frances noticed something out of place;
the remains of breakfast dishes cluttered the table: a bowl, a box of cereal, a mug, a spoon. The bowl was empty, but the mug was half full of
cold coffee; a sheen of oil floated on top.

Adrian had been interrupted just after breakfast but before he had
finished his coffee. She went back to the living room and sat down in
one of the tapestry-covered chairs, frustrated. So big a problem; so little
information. She thought back to her earlier observation about the cabin: identifying the genre was essential. Each had its peculiar protocols,
and if you didn't ask the right questions, the answers you got would be
either irrelevant or misleading.

So, she thought, this was a mystery, and she needed to ask questions
about motivation. The first possibility was that Adrian had left of his
own volition interrupted by a message or a messenger, with a summons
so urgent his morning coffee couldn't be finished. But what was so urgent that a man as organized as Adrian couldn't finish his coffee? Or
leave a message? The second possibility was that he had been abducted.
The room revealed no sign of a struggle, but that wasn't conclusive: he
could have been surprised at the door or compelled to leave by overwhelming odds or weapons.

She looked from the fireplace to the computer on the desk against
the opposite wall. She stood up and walked to it, released the catch, and
raised the monitor into place. She pushed the power button. When the
icons swam into view, she called up Adrian's files. A numbing array of
folders appeared on the screen. Adrian had been busy. The titles seemed

to describe reports related to his consulting business; a few of them seemed to deal with his plans to build a spaceship. She could come back to those later, if necessary.

She returned to the icons and clicked on his e-mail server. Unlike the programs themselves, this one required a password and clicking on "okay" did no good. She tried several passwords, including her name, her birthday (did Adrian know it?) and his, recalling that unlike Adrian she had sent him greetings on those occasions, "Winterbotham," "Cavendish," "stars," and "space." Then she tried "giftie," and the files opened.

There were a few messages waiting to be read, all dated in a two-day period that began six days earlier and ended four days earlier. The date Adrian disappeared and the date he had been eliminated from humanity's electronic memory? Frances scanned the messages; all but one related to Adrian's consulting business, and the remaining message said only "Haven't heard from you in a couple of days. Are you okay?" It was signed "Jessie."

The register was empty of messages sent and received earlier than six days previously. That was suspicious. Of course Adrian could have deleted his messages as they were read or sent, but that didn't make a lot of sense. At least some of the messages related to his business must have been worth keeping, but someone else, particularly someone in a hurry, would have deleted everything.

But what they might not have known was that deleted messages remained in the trash until they were squeezed out by new deletions. Frances was about to retrieve them when she was interrupted.

"What are you doing here?" a woman said.

———

Frances turned to see the shape of a woman outlined in the doorway. As the woman moved into the cabin with athletic grace, Frances noted with a pang that she was slender and dark-haired, and, with a sharper pang, young and attractive, in a tomboyish way. Frances pushed those feelings away: she would never be any of those things again.

"I might ask you the same question," Frances said.

"I'm Adrian's girlfriend."

Frances looked her up and down. She was dressed in jeans and a yellow t-shirt. Adrian was fifty-one, and this woman could not be more than, say, twenty-five. Frances could sense the young woman flushing under the scrutiny, but Frances didn't care. More was at stake than the feelings of a stranger. "I doubt that."

"Well," the woman said defiantly, "we're very close."

"For people who have never met," Frances guessed.

It must have been shrewd, because the young woman flinched. "We were e-mail correspondents. When he stopped responding, I decided I'd better check up."

"'Haven't heard from you in a couple of days. Are you okay?'" Frances quoted.

"How did you know?" the young woman asked.

Frances gestured at the laptop. "You look like a Jessie."

"That's me," the woman said. "Jessica Buhler."

"And you flew halfway across the country to check up on your e-mail friend?"

"How did you know?" Jessica said.

"You don't get a tan like that around here," Frances said. "Florida?"

"California. Near San Diego. But you haven't told me who you are."

"A real friend of Adrian's—Frances Farmstead. Like you I got concerned when I couldn't get in touch with Adrian, and I got really concerned when I discovered that he didn't exist."

"He didn't exist?"

"Not according to all the electronic records."

"No!" Jessica said. And then, "Adrian has mentioned you." Now it was Jessica's turn to appraise Frances. "He said you'd helped track down the author of the UFO book with the diagrams. That's how we got acquainted, on a serve-list for spaceship enthusiasts."

Frances wondered, for a moment, why she hadn't been included on such a list. "You don't look like a spaceship enthusiast."

"What does a spaceship enthusiast look like?"

"Strange," Frances said. "Like me."

"That's odd," Jessica said. Then, "I mean, why should someone who wants to build a spaceship be strange?"

"You look like someone who could get plenty of satisfaction right here," Frances said. "You wouldn't need to leave Earth."

"You don't know me. The question is—where is Adrian?" Jessica continued. She looked around the room as if he might be lurking somewhere.

"That's what a number of people would like to know. The government suspects aliens; I suspect the government."

"Aliens!" Jessica echoed.

"That's the way I said it," Frances responded. "Oh, aliens might have the motivation; they sent us a ticket to the stars and we cashed it in for creature comforts. They could be screwing things up, casting an occasional sabot in the machinery of our joy. But why send us a design if they're already here? And they sure aren't going to be interacting from a distance of dozens of light years. On the other hand, Adrian might be an annoyance to the people who don't want our peace disturbed."

Jessica stood as if poised between attack and flight. She had, apparently, never before considered either of these possibilities. "Aliens!" she said again. Then, heading for the door, she called over her shoulder, "Maybe that explains it."

"Explains what?" Frances called after her. When Jessie didn't reply, Frances trotted to catch up.

Jessica led the way to a meadow beyond the circle around the cabin that Frances had made before she entered. "This!" Jessica said, pointing.

Frances stood beside the young woman, panting. In front of them was a circle of burnt and blackened grass, about fifteen meters in diameter. Frances looked at it, puzzled.

"See?" Jessica said.

"You see," Frances said, absently, "but, as Sherlock Holmes said, you don't observe." What she couldn't see was the scenario this evidence fit. Oh, clearly it would fit an alien abduction category, but the questions to be asked seemed to hang in the air, unsupported, and to suggest no good answers. It was the wrong genre.

She looked up and started back toward the cabin, ignoring Jessica trotting along beside her, trying to talk about aliens, when she saw the smoke. She ran as fast as she could, but Jessica got there before her and stood looking at the flames already rising above the back of the cabin.

"My god!" Jessica said. Frances brushed past her. Jessica tried to grab her arm. "What are you doing?"

Frances ran to the front door, raised her arm across her face and over her mouth and nose, and went through the open front door. The room was filled with smoke pouring through the kitchen doorway. Frances felt her way to the desk. She grabbed for the computer. It was hot, and she almost dropped it as she picked it up, but she yanked it free from the cord plugged into a wall socket. She turned and staggered toward the front door.

As she was fumbling her way through the smoke, a hand reached out to guide her into the sunlight and the open air. She stood, shaking, gasping for breath, the laptop dangling from her right hand.

"That was crazy!" Jessica said.

"We had to have it," Frances said. "It was our only clue. And somebody wanted it destroyed."

"Or some *thing*," Jessica said.

———

They stood outside the Visitor Complex, the evening sun over their left shoulders, sinking toward the remote Gulf. They knew it was the Visitor Complex because the signs along Highway 3 had announced it for the past few miles, and the sign high on the building read:

KENNEDY SPACE CENTER

and under that

VISITOR COMPLEX.

But under that someone had stenciled:

ABANDONED IN PLACE

———

The entrance to the facility was overgrown by vegetation and cluttered with debris. The Space Center had indeed been abandoned and apparently for several years. A chain-link fence topped with barbed wire met the building on each side, and the doorway had been covered with plywood and nailed shut. Frances saw no way into the building or around it. Maybe Jessie could scale the fence, but Frances knew her limitations. And once they were inside, the Space Center was too big to cover on foot.

"Are you sure this is the place?" Jessie said.

"Clues never produce certainty," Frances said. "The detective accumulates evidence and plays hunches based on subconscious juggling of that evidence, like Perry Mason and Nero Wolfe."

"Who?" Jessie asked.

"Never mind. Anyway, we've been over this too often: Adrian was exchanging e-mails with people about alien spaceship design and petitioning the Energy Board for the resources to build one."

"And then there were those curious messages chastising humanity for not getting construction started," Jessie said.

"No way those could be from aliens," Frances said decisively. "Not in English. Not from the distance of the stars. Not signed 'KSC.' That could stand for a lot of things, but the most obvious meaning is 'Kennedy Space Center.'"

"Only it's abandoned."

"Just as the world has abandoned space," Frances said. "This has to be the place. It just feels right."

It had felt right all the way down from Atlanta in the rented car, to Macon on 75 and on 16 to Savannah and then down the coast on 95 to Jacksonville, Daytona Beach, and Cocoa, before switching to Highway 3 and heading back north to KSC. It had felt right when they passed a junkyard that looked like an old Emshwiller painting, with a Redstone rocket, several dilapidated rolling camera platforms, and the remains of what looked like a supersonic transport. A junkyard, that was what the space program had become, and now the facility that had made it possible had been abandoned in place.

The only thing that hadn't felt right was Jessie Buhler beside her all the way, talking, insisting that she couldn't go back to California without finding out what had happened to Adrian. But now here they stood, not far from what felt right, and they couldn't get in.

Still chattering, Jessie pried at the plywood without success. Finally she gave up in frustration. "If you're right about this place," she said, "there must be an entrance where people can *drive* in and out. They would need food and other supplies, and that requires frequent and easy access."

"They might use airplanes or helicopters," Frances said. "Landing strips may be abandoned, but they're still in place."

"People would notice air traffic," Jessie said. "But not a car or truck."

Frances looked at Jessie with a newfound respect.

"So let's look," Jessie said, getting back into the car.

They drove back to the road. The Space Center was on a barrier island between the mainland and the thin strip of beach that ran from Cape Canaveral down to Melbourne, with the Banana River on the east and the Indian River and a National Wildlife Refuge and its swamp on the west. One road entrance was overgrown with vines and clearly had not been used since the station was abandoned. An alligator was sunning itself on another, and nothing could persuade Frances to disturb it. A fallen tree blocked a third entrance, and a fourth, available only from Titusville, was cluttered with debris that may have been left when the Indian River overflowed or a hurricane had passed.

The entrance from Titusville was guarded by the omnipresent chain-link fence and a sliding chain-link gate with a drab beige booth beside it. Frances edged the car up to the gate, trying to avoid the worst of the debris. The gate looked rusty and dirty as if it hadn't been used in months or even years. "Take a look," she told Jessie.

"Why me?" Jessie asked.

"You're younger and quicker," Frances said.

Carefully searching the ground before each step, Jessie finally reached the gate. She looked back. "It's locked," she said.

"Give it a yank anyway," Frances said.

Jessie pulled at something Frances couldn't see and then turned around holding something in the air. "Either it was broken or only meant to look locked."

"The power must have been shut off long ago. Push the gate open," Frances said.

Jessie pushed. The gate slid back smoothly as if it had been oiled recently. "Looks like you were right," she said, as Frances rolled the car through the opened gateway and Jessie got back inside.

"Either that or someone else is holed up here," Frances said. She stopped the car on the other side of the gate. "You'd better shut it."

"Not me," Jessie said, shivering. "I hate wild animals. And anyway, we may need to leave in a hurry."

They headed across what once had been a bustling complex specializing in hurling men toward the moon. Now it was a vast, silent sea of concrete in which their car moved like a tiny bottle tossed into the ocean.

Only it wasn't empty. Weeds, some of them as tall as bushes, had grown up in cracks. Little brown wild pigs scattered in front of them as the car approached, and here and there a wild boar snorted at them, trotting from behind a building to assert its territorial rights. Armadillos lifted their heads from their inspection of the ground and sidled away when the car got close; alligators didn't seem to care, although they heard a distant roar. Vines and small trees reached from the Indian River to reclaim the land from civilization's efforts to pave it into submission. Woodpeckers pounded trees for insects. Rattlesnakes sunned themselves on ledges and in empty patches of concrete. Eagles soared overhead, and occasionally, winging through the darkening sky, a snowy egret. Insects splattered against the windshield and threatened to invade the interior through closed windows.

"When they say 'abandoned,'" Jessie said, "they meant returned to nature and the native populations. It certainly doesn't look as if anybody has been here."

"Don't forget the gate," Frances said, but she looked lost as well. Where on these roads, among these enigmatic structures, would a band of kidnappers hide?

She felt the abandonment of this place, the loss of purpose that the buildings and the stretches of concrete had once symbolized, the bustle of people and vehicles that had expressed the human will to conquer space, the roar of massive engines that had shouted their defiance at the Earth that kept its offspring tied to its apron strings.

Over on the Cape side, a couple of hundred yards from the beach and the blue Atlantic Ocean beyond, were the remains of a launch pad. Half a dozen twenty-foot concrete and metal arms supported a doughnut ring of concrete and exposed metal. The metal parts wore a patina of age and despair. An "abandoned in place" sign was stenciled on one of the slabs. Another slab had a plaque attached to it. Frances didn't get close enough to read what it said. The entire place filled her with melancholy, like a Space Age Stonehenge raised to forgotten gods, and the plaque, she had the feeling, was inscribed with the names of ancient heroes.

Frances pulled to a stop, with their backs to the ocean, facing the vast Space Center complex with its roads and runways and buildings. "I don't know where to look," she said. "We could spend a week here and still not exhaust the possibilities."

"What about that place?" Jessie said, motioning toward a huge square structure that towered in the middle of the Center, dominating the entire complex. "It's big enough to hide a small city."

"That must be where they assembled the big rockets," Frances said. "Well, why not?"

She headed back toward the massive building. It loomed even bigger as they approached, until the top reaches seemed to disappear into the blue sky. Most of it was white with darker panels. As they got closer, they could see some low outbuildings. On one side a gigantic American flag, perhaps two hundred feet tall, had been painted. Then came a dark panel inset with a lighter rectangle and, on the other side, a huge NASA symbol, once dark blue, now faded. Temporary structures surrounding the building had deteriorated and some had fallen apart, but the main building still seemed solid and as resistant to time as a latter-day Great Pyramid.

Another chain-link fence surrounded the building, and turnstiles guarded the entrance. One of them had broken, however, and lay on its side beside the fence, its metal pipes reaching helplessly toward the sky, the entrance it had once sealed gaping beside it.

"The Vehicle Assembly Building," Frances said, as if that were the answer to a crossword puzzle. "The VAB. That's what they used to call it. Shall we go in?" She got out of the car without waiting for an answer.

The doorway to the VAB had been covered by plywood, but the wood, like the turnstile, had fallen away, leaving a dark, forbidding rectangle. Frances stepped through gingerly, Jessie following closely behind.

Inside the building, rain was falling. Frances waited just inside the doorway until her vision returned. Light filtered from louvers high above, shining through the mist of descending rain and the clouds that had formed in the remote upper reaches of the vast spaces enclosed there. When the shower eased, Frances could see the inside of the building, though the far walls and the distant ceiling faded into gray nothing.

She felt again as if she were in a cathedral built for an outworn worship. She shook herself and began noticing details: a wide avenue traversed the middle and on each side platforms, catwalks, what seemed like elevators, and cranes, a lot of them, and two huge cranes high above that crossed a gulf.

"Adrian!" she called out in desperation, knowing that they could never exhaust the hiding places in this incredible structure. The name echoed back to her from near and far, rolling around the cavernous interior and returning to her moment by moment.

"Please don't do that again," Jessie whispered. "It sounds so mournful. Like a lament for the dead."

———

Frances moved down the wide thoroughfare that ran through the middle of the building. Tools and leaves and other debris were scattered across what once must have been scrubbed as clean as her kitchen floor. In the distance loomed a tall structure. As Frances got closer, she realized that it was a rocket on a platform, solid boosters attached to an external tank. She craned her neck to look up at the top. All it needed, she realized, was a space shuttle and transportation to a launching pad and it could be launched.

"What is it?" Jessie asked.

"Either a rocket that was abandoned when the rest of the place was shut down," Frances said, "or something that a bunch of amateurs are trying to cobble together from left-over parts. Either way, anybody would be out of their mind to trust their lives to it."

Her words echoed less stridently from the partitions around them. For a moment they obscured the noises someone was making on a nearby catwalk. Then they heard footsteps. Coming closer. Jessie squeezed Frances' upper arm. Frances did not turn around.

"That's right," someone said. "It's an exercise in faith, like lighting a votary candle."

"Adrian?" Frances said.

"You've found me," a voice said softly.

Frances turned. Adrian looked much the same as she had seen him last—was it four years ago? Maybe a little older around the eyes, a little grayer around the edges. But his blue eyes were still as steadfast and concerned. "Adrian!" she said. "You've put us to a great deal of bother. Why didn't you let us know?"

Adrian spread his hands in a universal gesture of helplessness. The gesture also happened to indicate the space around them. Occupying that space, a few paces away, were four men and a woman, dressed in white, uniform-like coveralls. Frances had been so focused on Adrian's footsteps that the approach of the others had gone unnoticed. They looked grim and determined, a bit like Adrian himself when he was thinking about spaceships.

"They talked me out of it," Adrian said.

"I suppose they were the ones who came and took you away," Frances said. Adrian nodded. "Against your will?"

Adrian hesitated. "Against my better judgment."

"Which means," Frances said, "that they had been in touch with you earlier, and that you had disagreed about the next procedure."

"They were—persuasive," Adrian said. "Not that I was opposed to their goals. Only their methods."

"They're space-nuts, too?" Her epithet concealed a deeper pain. What was there in a few humans that yearned for liberation? Was it the eternal wanderlust or something deeper?

"Including someone I want you to meet," Adrian said. He turned toward the steep stairs down which he had come.

Standing at their foot was a man in slacks and jacket who looked familiar. "Cavendish?" Frances said.

The man nodded.

"Last time I saw you was in Menninger's Clinic in Topeka," Frances said.

"I was cured," Cavendish said simply. "With the help of some biogenetic materials."

"But not cured, apparently, of your interest in alien spaceship designs," Frances said.

Cavendish fidgeted. "Not of that," he said.

"Careful, Frances," Adrian said. "He still gets agitated."

Cavendish held up a hand. "That's okay." But his head began to twitch.

"Did you figure it out?" Frances asked.

"Frances!" Adrian cautioned.

"Why they sent the designs?" Frances continued.

Cavendish held out his hands to show that they were steady. "That's the question, isn't it? Why did they send the designs? Why didn't they just come here? What do they want from us?"

"And the fact that there are no answers doesn't bother you anymore?" Frances asked.

"Of course it bothers me. But I can think clearly now, and I understand that there are answers. We won't find them, however, until we build the ship and go where the answers are. That's the only way we can find peace." His breath came out at the end, in an explosive rush, as if he had been holding it in all the time he spoke.

"That's the way it is," Frances said. She motioned toward the partially assembled rocket. "But you don't intend to go anywhere in that, I hope."

"That's just for practice," Cavendish said. "When we finally get the resources to build the ship, we'll need experience, won't we? So we sneak a little power, at night, when nobody's paying attention."

"And how is all this going to get you anywhere?" Frances asked. This time she was speaking to Adrian.

"I don't know," Adrian said.

"Did you know that they removed all proof of your existence?" Frances said. " At least the electronic part."

Adrian looked accusingly at Cavendish. "You didn't!"

Cavendish shrugged. His head had stopped twitching. "We were practicing again. One strategy we have considered is to make ourselves sufficiently irritating that the Energy Board will protect itself."

"With the pearl of space?" Adrian asked.

"What about the power stoppages?" Frances said. "The sabotage? The upsurge in violent crime?"

Cavendish looked surprised. "Not us! But that would add to the irritant factor."

"I've noticed a few outages," Adrian said, "but I thought—"

"It was normal," Frances concluded. "Right. But Makepeace doesn't."

"Makepeace?"

"He's working for the Energy Board now. He wanted me to find you. He says there's a lot of unusual activity going on that nobody notices because of the good times."

"Shouldn't you introduce me to your companion?" Adrian said. "What's she doing here?"

Jessie stepped from behind Frances looking a bit sheepish. "I'm Jessie."

Adrian raised his eyebrows. "Yes?"

"Jessica Buhler."

"Who is Jessica Buhler?" Adrian asked.

Frances turned accusingly toward Jessie, but before she could say anything they heard the roar of jets outside.

———

The distant entrance to the Vehicle Assembly Building was filled with tiny black figures. Frances looked around. The coveralled space-nuts had disappeared and so had Cavendish.

"Why did you do it?" Frances asked Jessie.

"Why blame me?" Jessie said defiantly. "Maybe that man—Makepeace—put a tracer on you!"

"You're the plant," Frances said. "Why?"

Jessie looked contrite. "All right, I might as well admit it. When I started, it was just another job, and by the time I got involved it was too late."

"Involved?" Frances said.

"If I'd known—" Jessie said. "If I'd known you—and Adrian and what was at stake—"

"You set the fire?" Frances said accusingly.

"Not me," Jessie protested. "Maybe somebody else." She took a ragged breath. "What I found out is that I'd like to build a spaceship. I wish I could be one of you," she said softly. "I know it's too late, but that's what I'd like."

Frances noted the way Jessie looked at Adrian and felt a pang of jealousy. There was something attractive about a man who cared more about an idea than about relationships.

Adrian had been looking back and forth between the two of them. "We've got to get out of here," he said. He motioned toward where the black figures had turned into people, men and women, in form-fitting gray uniforms. They were approaching rapidly, spread out across the broad aisle like a military outfit, trotting.

Frances shook her head. "That never works," she said. "In the movies and the TV shows, the pursuers always catch up. Sometimes the culprits get away temporarily, but they get caught in the end, and that's when people get hurt."

"This isn't the movies, Frances," Adrian said.

"I know, Adrian, but movies are a lot easier to understand. A lot of wisdom has been written and filmed, and you might as well take advantage of other people's analyses. Anyway, your friends or kidnappers— Cavendish and his crew—ought to have a chance to escape."

"That's true," Adrian admitted. "But what about—?" He nodded in the direction of Jessie.

"I've done all the betraying I'm going to do," Jessie said.

"Good," Frances said.

The people in the gray uniforms, looking like clones of the ill-matched twins who had sprung into Frances' store the day before, surrounded them. There were eight of them. Even as young and athletic as they seemed, they were breathing hard.

"Welcome to the Vehicle Assembly Building," Frances said. "May I show you around? Those are bridge cranes, those big ones up there, and over there, that is an external tank mated to a pair of solid-rocket boosters but without, I am sorry to say, the orbiter—"

"Which one of you is Adrian Mast?" one of the women asked.

"I'm Adrian Mast," Adrian said.

"You'll come with us," the woman said. She was tall and slender but she held herself like an acrobat.

"By whose authority?" Adrian asked.

"By the authority of the Energy Board."

"The Energy Board has no police powers."

"This is an administrative action taken to prevent an interruption in service."

Adrian looked at Frances. "Shall we go?"

Frances stepped forward. "You'll have to take me, too," she said.

"I have no orders—" the woman began.

"Me, too," Jessie said.

The woman shrugged. "Come with us." She turned and the three of them followed her out down the long, broad aisle toward the entrance, the other uniformed personnel slightly behind them like an honor guard.

A jet helicopter stood outside the VAB, its rotors idling. It was painted Energy Board gray with a silver lightning bolt on the nose. So was a small jet airplane parked beside the helicopter. The honor guard escorted them to the airplane and their leader motioned them up the lowered stairs. After their brief exposure to Florida sunshine, the interior seemed dark, and even darker after the stairs were raised behind them, closing them into the ship. Almost immediately, it began to taxi.

As her eyes adjusted to the interior, Frances noticed the skeletal man sitting in a swiveling leather chair a few feet away. "Makepeace," she said. "Why am I not surprised?"

"Frances," Makepeace said, "you'd better be seated. We'll be taking off soon. And Adrian. And Jessica."

"You know Jessie?" Frances said, seating herself opposite Makepeace, while Adrian took a seat beside her and Jessie, the one beside Makepeace.

"She's one of my best," Makepeace said.

Jessie looked embarrassed.

"Though perhaps no longer," Makepeace said.

"I quit," Jessie said.

The airplane turned and almost immediately accelerated and within a few hundred yards lifted its nose into the sky. When the cabin had quieted down, Adrian asked, "What is all this about?"

"The Energy Board wants to speak to you," Makepeace said.

"Why?"

"Maybe they wish to sponsor your spaceship."

"Why should they do that? Why now? Why in person?"

Makepeace folded his hands together over his stomach. It may have been a gesture left over from the days when he had an ample belly on which to rest them. "The Energy Board gets nervous when something unpredictable happens. There have been outages, outbreaks, violence, your disappearance. What if they are linked?"

"In what way?"

Makepeace shrugged. "The Energy Board may have other sources of information. Maybe not. Maybe they hope you will be able to provide some. Maybe they hope you will give them wise counsel."

Adrian laughed. Frances was proud of him.

When the plane was over the African coastline, the engines suddenly cut off.

———

Frances clenched the arms of her seat as her body attempted to fly. The gentle vibration that had become a part of their existence was gone. "What's going on?" she said, trying to steady her voice.

"One of those outages Makepeace mentioned," Adrian said.

The compartment was eerily silent. "You mean," Frances said, "this plane operates by broadcast power?"

Adrian nodded. "And steam. But there must be a backup—"

Just then the engines sputtered and caught, cut out, and caught again. The airplane steadied, pressing them back into their seats, and began climbing toward its lost altitude.

Adrian pointed out the window toward the right-hand engine. "The exhaust isn't steam anymore. We're flying on fuel reserves."

A woman's voice came over the speaker. "Everybody okay back there?"

"Okay," Makepeace said.

"Sorry about the power loss," the voice said. "We're shifting back to broadcast power. We should be at our destination in half an hour."

Frances looked down into the dark continent below. The moon was full, but the land was still only scantily visible. If the sun had been shining she could have seen the green of West Africa, restored in only a few years to nearly its virgin state before the rape of European empire builders. If she had been able to see farther, she might have observed modern cities rising to the north and south, and if she had been able to see beneath the jungle canopies, villages with air-conditioned huts, multi-channeled television sets, and modern schools.

The blessings of alien technology had been bestowed with a lavish and indiscriminate hand. Half an hour later the plane swiveled its engines and lowered itself, in the night, onto a landing pad on top of Kilimanjaro.

They were ushered through corridors and anterooms into a large office. One wall flamed with the disk of the sun. Frances had to turn her head to shut down the glare until the man at the clean, transparent desk waved his hand and the image dimmed. How appropriate, Frances thought, that this structure, raised to the sun, should display on its office wall the source of its power, which this man could control like Apollo scattering largess to mere mortals.

The man at the desk introduced himself as the Energy Board Chair for Africa. His office was large and eclectic. His desk, fashioned from clear plastic, occupied one corner, and old-fashioned maroon-leather chairs surrounded a clear-plastic conference table. But the floors were covered with multi-colored African throw rugs, and spears and a bark shield hung upon the wall opposite the mural. The anomaly was the absence of windows as if what happened inside the room was more important than anything outside.

"You think of me as powerful," the Chairman said from behind his bare desk, which itself symbolized his ability to command service, "but I am a mere functionary, no more important than a conduit." He was a large man with big shoulders and a torso spreading around the middle; he wasn't a man that anyone would call a "functionary."

"More like a switch," Frances said, "that can be turned on or off, as during our flight."

"That was not our doing," the Chairman said.

"For someone without power," Adrian said, "having people summoned from halfway around the world displays real persuasion."

"You are not here of your own free will?" the Chairman asked. "You felt coerced?"

Adrian looked at Frances and then at Jessie standing a foot or two behind. "It didn't seem wise to refuse."

"I must speak to my emissaries," the Chairman said. "I apologize for any intimidation you may have felt, but the matter seemed urgent." He waved a black hand at them. He seemed good at that, as if he was used to waving a hand and accomplishing miracles. "But first, let me say that you should be pleased with what you accomplished a decade ago."

"It worked out okay, didn't it?" Adrian said cautiously.

"Better than it had any right," the Chairman said. "Your instincts were correct, and those who feared that cheap power would upset the world's precarious political balance were wrong."

"As they often are," Frances said.

The Chairman sighed. "True. Responsibility shrivels the imagination and enfeebles the will."

"While we who have little to lose can dream wildly and act boldly," Adrian said.

"Just so. Won't you sit?" The Chairman waved a hand at the conference table. "Join me in some refreshments?"

"Coffee, perhaps," Frances said. She sank into a chair facing the muraled wall, expecting to see black moths encircling the sun and maybe the outline of a shark. Cups of coffee appeared almost instantly, served by silent young men and women in gray uniforms. "It's been a long day."

Adrian sat next to her; Jessie sat opposite. Jessie had been silent since the first moments on the airplane, contemplating her sins, perhaps, and how she might atone. Makepeace had been left behind in the anteroom, but Jessie, for some reason, had been allowed to accompany them.

The Chairman eased his large body into the chair at the head of the table, like a tribal chief into a throne. He inclined his head. "We want you to understand that we recognize you as the architects of this world."

"We?" Frances echoed.

"The other chairs and I."

"We may have given it a shove," Adrian said. "No more. We didn't design it."

"No," the Chairman said, "what you designed was a spaceship. Like this." He waved his hand, and the mural on the wall opposite transformed itself into a view screen with a close up of the sun's surface. It was a scene Frances had viewed before. The black moths that were the alien-designed photon collectors were fluttering in front of the sun and then the outline of a ship ghosted across.

"Like that, but not that," Adrian said.

"You had nothing to do with it?" the Chairman asked.

"No," Adrian said, "and you could have found that out without bring-ing us halfway around the world."

"But then," the Chairman said, "I wouldn't have been able to look into your faces when you said it."

"A dubious pleasure," Frances said.

"But maybe you consider yourself a judge of veracity," Adrian said.

"Would I be sitting here if I weren't?" the Chairman asked. "The problem we face is: if not you, who? And how?"

Frances looked toward Adrian and then back at the Chairman. "I think of it," she said, "as a reminder. Of a broken promise."

"We made no promises," the Chairman said.

"The promise was implicit," Frances said. "We get designs that we could not have developed on our own—"

"At least at this stage in our technological development," Adrian added.

"—And we'll build a spaceship," Frances continued. "We've taken the designs and applied the energy source to Earth's problems. They've worked better than anyone expected."

"The petty squabblings over wealth and its unequal distribution have diminished to almost nothing," Adrian said. "The age of peace and plen-ty are at hand."

The Chairman looked pained. "Then why do we have these outbreaks of violence, divorce, sabotage...?"

"Makepeace told me about that," Frances said, "I didn't tell him what I thought was behind it: human perversity."

"Perversity?"

"The species didn't survive by getting fat and happy," Frances said. "When times get too easy, humanity starts making trouble for itself."

"There have hardly been enough fat and happy times in human his-tory to test that hypothesis," the Chairman said. "In any case, the unrest is not species-wide."

"Like talent of any kind," Adrian said, "it emerges sporadically and unpredictably, but it emerges all the same."

"And even with the rest," Frances said, "let individual lives get too un-eventful and people will move, quit jobs, start affairs, get divorced...."

"Ask them about the aliens," a voice said from the direction of the wall screen, as if the sun itself had spoken.

———

The Chairman moved his magical hand and the sun disappeared to be replaced by a screen segmented into four. In each segment was a different person: a slender Asian woman in a silk gown, a plump white male in a business suit, a youthful-looking man with a brown face, wearing a casual white jacket, and a middle-aged woman in gray slacks and blazer.

"These are the other Chairs," the Chairman said. He did not offer to introduce them, and it was an indication of their anonymity in this uneventful world that Frances knew none of them. She knew only that, like the Chair for Africa, they occupied sites on the tops of mountains, where atmospheric losses of power beamed from satellites were minimal and terrestrial broadcast was easiest.

"Ask them about the aliens," the Asian woman said again.

"Are aliens behind these events?" the Chairman asked.

"That wouldn't make sense," Adrian said. "Why would they send us designs for a spaceship if they were already here?"

"To deceive us?" the man with the brown face suggested.

"And give us a power system that could fuel a ship to the stars—or a world to peace and plenty?" Adrian said. He shook his head.

"Beware of aliens bearing gifts," said the plump man in the white suit.

"Maybe they're acting from a distance," the woman in slacks and blazer suggested.

"At the distance of the stars, even the nearest of them?" Frances said. "No way they could find out what was going on here, much less act in time to be effective."

"Agents?" the Asian woman suggested.

Jessie spoke for the first time. "They do have agents," she said. Everyone turned toward her in surprise. Even the faces on the wall seemed to look in her direction. "They're the agents of an idea, and the idea is spaceflight. Freedom. Answering the call. There's nothing as transforming as an idea."

"She's right," Adrian said. "What you have is what seems to be a single phenomenon with multiple causes. One of them is the space community that wants to build a spaceship and find out what the aliens want. Another is the restless element of society that can't stand good times. There may be others. The spaceflight group deleted evidence of my existence. Another group is behind the power outages, probably by computer viruses."

"But there is a solution," Frances said.

The faces turned back in her direction.

"You can ride it out," Frances said, "and maybe that is the least risky option. The space-nuts will get old and die off. The malcontents can be rooted out and punished. But the final result may be a species that has lost its soul."

"Humanity can't go to the stars when it can't afford it," Adrian said, "and when it can afford it, humanity has no incentive to go. The apparent paradise on Earth may actually be a dead end. The malcontents may be the true spirit of humanity—always looking for something they haven't got."

"The other option?" the Chairman asked.

"Let them go!" Jessie said.

Adrian looked at her, and said with growing enthusiasm, "She's right. Give the space-nuts the resources to build a ship and offer the malcontents an opportunity to sign on. That's always worked for humanity, as long as there was another world to discover, another frontier to pioneer."

"It wouldn't cost you much," Frances said. "The energy moths are self-replicating and by the time construction on the spaceship gets going you won't know what to do with all the excess energy."

"Materials can be mined in space," Adrian said. "Asteroids. Comets. Hydrogen from Jupiter for reaction mass, if that is needed."

"Let us go," Jessie said.

"Us?" Frances echoed.

"I want to go, too."

"But what about the aliens?" the oriental woman asked.

"We'll never know, will we?" Frances said. "Until we go."

"Do we risk something by going?" Adrian continued. "The people who go risk a lot. The people who stay behind risk a bit less, but still enough to concern them. Maybe the designs are a trick, some nefarious plot to trap humanity. But they've made us stronger; they've unified us by removing the inequalities that kept us apart. So not going is a bigger risk."

The faces on the wall seemed to exchange glances with the Chairman before he waved his hand and they disappeared to be replaced by the image of the sun. "The one function we have," the Chairman said, "is to transmit power. We have decided that you should have it." He held up his hand as they started to speak. "Your argument about ridding ourselves of the malcontents was persuasive. We have no desire to contact aliens, no aspirations for the transcendental. We are content to be no more than we are, the transmitters of power to those who need it, the conservators of human happiness."

"You have conserved our happiness," Frances said.

The Chairman waved his hand once more at the wall, and once more it responded with the sun girdled by energy-absorbing black moths. And when the design for the spaceship ghosted across the screen, it seemed to those who watched that it was already transforming itself into something substantial enough to carry humanity to the stars.

Shape has no shape, nor will your thinking shape it;
Space has no confines; and no borders time.
And yet, to think the abyss is to escape it.

CONRAD AIKEN, SONNET XXVI

⊢⊣

Part Three

THE ABYSS

JESSICA BUHLER LOOKED UP FROM THE SEAM on the cigar-shaped spaceship whose far end, like the horizon, hid what lay beyond. A hand-held electronic weld-checker, secured by a safety cord, dangled from the glove of her spacesuit. The ship had been put together from oddly shaped pieces of metal, like a child's puzzle, and the job of checking thousands of seams might never be done. The devices that sealed the seams checked welds as they were made, but when survival depended on every part and every person functioning perfectly, Adrian believed in checking and rechecking. That was his nature, Jessica knew, but it also was a measure of his commitment to the mission he had chosen. Before she was born, she amended. It was important to keep matters in perspective.

Beneath her was the long hull of the spaceship, apparently complete but as yet untested against the forces of acceleration. Frances Farmstead would have identified the genre as 1930s science fiction. She could tell, she would have said, because the ship looked as if it had been lifted from the cover of *Astounding Stories*, maybe the first installment of *The Skylark of Valeron*. Images that endure, she said, characterize situations better than rational analysis. They encapsulated the wisdom of the species.

Some of the crew laughed at Frances and her genres. "How'd them

61

aliens get hold of a copy of *Astounding*?" they'd say. But Frances was unperturbed. "If you don't identify the situation, you won't know what to do when it comes time to act," she said, and she was so sure of herself that some of them began to wonder if she might be right.

But building the ship hadn't been as easy as the stories made it sound. There was none of this "they all pitched in and by working hard they put the ship together in a few weeks," or "they built the ship in an empty barn by working after school and on weekends."

Jessica was attached to the smooth metal surface by magnetic grapples as she moved, with her machine, from seam to seam. When she raised her head she could see the blue, cloud-strewn globe of the Earth disturbingly above, and then, in a gut-wrenching transformation, like some inescapable abyss yawning below. She closed her eyes and mentally readjusted her relationship to the universe. It was an exercise in which they all had grown skillful—all except Frances who, in spite of her experience in identifying situations according to the genre models that came to her so readily, had been space-sick until the chemists and physicians found a medicine that worked. Even then Frances had never been able to labor outside where the need to invent one's own orientation had left her dizzy and disturbed.

Past the far end of the ship Jessica could see the skeleton of the old space station, half its parts scavenged for structural elements and hull plates. Like the Kennedy Space Center from which they had boosted into orbit, the space station had been abandoned in place. At first the construction workers who would become the crew had lived in the quarters that once had housed astronauts and experiments. As soon as they had settled in, the station itself, trembling in all its fragile connections, had been raised from its degraded orbit by rocket motors carefully placed to minimize stress. Only afterward, as people considered the difficulty of constructing the ship that would house the alien-designed equipment and of boosting into orbit the necessary parts, did someone suggest supplementing what had to be manufactured below with materials already available. The first part of the spaceship built, then, was the crew's living quarters. In the alien designs those spaces had been left blank, as if the aliens had understood that creatures who received their message were likely to come in many shapes and sizes. It was an issue frequently discussed over the mess table and in late night bull-sessions: what did it mean that the aliens made no assumptions about the physiology of sentience?

Nobody wept over the deconstruction of the space station except a few sentimentalists who had pinned their hopes for space on this stepping-stone to the stars. That would once have included Jessica and the head of the project, Adrian Mast, and the ageless Frances, his adviser and co-conspirator. But that had been fifteen years earlier, when all this started in a book found by Adrian on a UFO remainder table. Five years earlier the Energy Board had given them the power, but that left the would-be space-travelers dependent upon their own manpower and the construction workers they could recruit. The number of volunteers had surprised them, but all this, and their training, had taken a year, and the construction itself, another four years.

Part of the resources allotted to them was the space station. In another form it might, indeed, reach the stars. If the alien designs worked. That was the immediate concern. What would happen when the button was pushed? Would the containment vessel work or would the ship simply disappear in a titanic union of matter and antimatter? Would the ship disintegrate under acceleration? If it moved, would it move at interstellar speeds? Could they control it? Could their bodies endure it? If everything worked properly, where would they go and how long would the voyage take?

Those were the questions that worried Adrian, even if he didn't show it. They worried Cavendish, who fretted about it all the time until everybody told him to shut up. And it worried Frances most of all, although she concealed it from Adrian and everybody else. She couldn't conceal it from Jessica, however; nothing can be concealed between two women who love the same man, and everything is obscure to the man who is so wrapped up in his job that he has no time for personal relationships.

All this passed through Jessica's mind in the fleeting moment of relaxation and attitude adjustment before the terrible realization hit her that the ship had begun to tremble beneath her feet.

———

"What's going on?" she said into the suit radio she had activated with her chin. The receiver only crackled as if someone had leaned against the on-switch. By that time Jessica had slipped the seam-checker into magnetic catches on her suit and was running across the outer hull, breaking one magnetic grapple free and swinging it ahead, and then the other, in an unconscious coordination of movements that she had perfected over the past years. "What's happening?" she asked again. Unfortunately, she was almost as far as she could get from the nearest open hatch. By the time she was halfway there, her body had tightened with the notion that the ship had begun to move. She looked back over her shoulder. It was a contortion in the airtight suit made possible only by her slender athleticism. The skeleton of the space station seemed farther away. It was all subjective, she told herself, and then she was at the hatch and pulling herself into it, locking the hatch door in place with another athletic contortion, and waiting for the air pressure to build to the point where the inner door could be unlocked.

She backed into the clamps that held a row of spacesuits just inside the inner hatchway. It was a slow process, but faster than trying to maneuver down narrow corridors in a bulky suit and then being unable to communicate except by radio. Finally she was free. Dressed in what looked like a one-piece garment of long underwear, she propelled herself down a zero-gravity corridor toward the forward control room. It was like a high-platform dive without an entry, a repetition in which she caught herself with bent knees at a turn and launched herself again until she arrived, at last, at a room crowded with dials and screens and computers and keyboards and distraught people milling about aimlessly and weightlessly.

Adrian was among them and Frances and Peter and a dozen or more others whose names and faces had become as familiar to her as neighborhood buddies. Some of them hung upside down or sideways to her orientation, but that surrealistic panorama no longer had the power to surprise. She had no time now to identify them individually. "What's going on?" she asked again.

They looked at her, in every possible configuration. "Someone programmed an engine test into the control-room computer," Adrian said. "Fortunately, there were only a few atoms of antimatter in the containment vessel—maybe a billion or so—left over from the preinstallation tests. And only a similar femtogram of matter. Otherwise it might have been catastrophic."

"We didn't move," Frances said. "Just shuddered."

"Who did it?" Jessica asked.

Frances shrugged.

"No way to know," Adrian said. "We don't even know how it was done."

"But you said a test was programmed into the control-room computer?" Jessica said.

"That's the only way the engine could be started," Adrian said. "The entire process is so complex that the human mind can't perform the necessary calculations or react quickly enough. We'll check the computer programs, but I suspect that whoever was clever enough to install the program so that it nestled, unsuspected, among the computer's legitimate programming, won't have left any digital fingerprints."

"At least," Peter said nervously, "we know that the engines work."

"We knew that already," Adrian said. "From the static tests."

"But we didn't know if the mountings would hold or the ship would blow up." A muscle twitched near Peter's left eye.

"We still don't know," Adrian said.

"Some people have said they saw the bearded man," Frances said.

"The bearded man," Jessica repeated.

The bearded man had become a legend within the crew. Ever since workmen had taken up residence within the space station, one person or another had reported brief glimpses of a strange man. He was described by each of the viewers as wiry in appearance, with skin burnt nearly black by space radiation, against which an unkempt white beard was even more spectacular. The sightings were so fleeting or so isolated that no verification was possible. As difficult as it was to imagine a mysterious person existing within the closed community of space workers, some people were beginning to believe in him; others thought he was a ghost or maybe a mass hallucination brought on by concern about their work and its risks, or the brooding presence of the aliens and all the unanswered questions they trailed behind them.

"We'll put our best people to work analyzing the computer data," Adrian said, "and providing safeguards against future sabotage."

"Sabotage?" Jessica asked. "You think it was sabotage?"

"It certainly seems like it, but we can't let it interfere with our mission or it will have succeeded. Let's get back to finishing up. Tomorrow we load antimatter and reaction mass, and the day after that we take our first test-flight. Everything has to be ready by then."

"You haven't said yet who's going to be on board during the test flight," Peter said.

"Everybody who wants to be," Adrian said. "Anyone who doesn't want to share the risks can back out if they wish, with no hard feelings. We'll let them board afterward."

"And what if it blows up?" Peter asked.

"Then we'll all go with it," Adrian said. "We might as well face reality: This is our only chance. The Energy Board won't give us another. Who wants to survive their dreams?"

Jessica turned from the door into the control room to head back to her lonely job of checking seams. They were airtight, that had been clear ever since the crew moved in, but suddenly it seemed vitally important that they hold up under acceleration.

"Jessie," Frances said, coming after her. "Can we talk?"

As soon as they had reached a point beyond earshot of the others,

Frances stopped Jessica with a hand on her arm. "You asked who did it," Frances said. "Some members of the crew think it was you."

———

Jessica looked at Frances, wondering why the old woman who was her unlikely rival was telling her this. "Why would anyone think that?"

"You were Makepeace's agent," Frances said. "People remember."

"I've worked five years on this project," Jessica said. "How long does it take to earn people's trust?"

Frances gestured as if to say, "People have long memories." And "Look at you—young and shapely and pretty. How can anyone who isn't any of those things be sure what people like you would do?" The movement made her spin gently until Jessica reached out a hand to stop her and relieve Frances' nervous inner ears. Unlike the revealing long underwear most of them wore, Frances was wearing loose coveralls; although biogenetic treatment had removed fat and years, it could not change the fact that she was short and sturdy.

"Anyway," Jessica said, "why would I want to sabotage the ship when I was out checking seams?"

"I didn't say it was reasonable," Frances said. "I just thought you ought to know what people were saying."

"I'm sure they're saying the same thing about everybody, with the possible exception of Adrian," Jessica said. "Nobody's above suspicion, and even Adrian might be trying to test the crew."

"Or get rid of people he doesn't trust by assigning them to duties on the hull," Frances said, "at the time of the test."

"While we're at it," Jessica said, "we might as well throw in the bearded man."

"Him, too."

"Well," Jessica said, spinning toward the distant hatchway, "at least I know you set them straight. About me."

"You know I did," Frances called after her.

But Jessica carried her suspicions back onto the hull and her lonely job. Was it ever going to end? Would she always be an outsider?

At the end of her long shift, tired and hungry and still brooding over Frances' subtle accusation, she straightened up from the last seam and took one final look around. The next day she would be loading antimatter and who knew whether some accident would destroy all their work and hopes and them as well. The following day, if all went without disaster, they would make a test run. However matters went, there would not be many more chances to stand free above the abyss and consider her birth planet, a blue, water-blessed oasis in the vast desert of space. She looked at it steadily for several minutes, thinking warm thoughts of home and family and favorite things, before she sighed, secured her equipment to the magnetic catches on the suit, and turned toward the nearest hatch.

Only then did she think about the bearded man and swung around to face the ruins of the space station, looking like the archeological remains of a curiously shaped dinosaur. On an impulse she moved to a portion of the ship closest to the former station and launched herself into the dark desert she had just been considering. She made a small adjustment of her steering jets and caught a girder on the station as she passed. That sort of space maneuvering had become commonplace in the past four years, although some of the crew were better at it than others and a few, like Frances, never did it at all.

Jessica swung herself along the girder until she reached a portion of the station that still retained a few plates. There she used her magnetic grapples to walk toward the part of the station that was relatively untouched. In the middle of a solid metal wall was a hatch that she didn't remember, that had no business still being there. She cycled it open. Beyond was darkness, and, from the lack of condensation when the hatch opened, airlessness as well. Her suit lights revealed a storeroom in which discarded equipment and tools floated like a Dalí nightmare. She shut the door behind her, to keep the debris from cluttering nearby orbit, and made her way through this obstacle course to the far wall where another closed hatch waited to be opened.

She hesitated. Why had no one been here before? Or if they had been here, why had they left the equipment loose behind them and why were the hatches closed? But then, before further doubts could damage her resolve, she reached forward to palm the hatch switch.

The hatch opened. A gush of ice particles rushed past her helmet as moisture from the air within froze instantly. Jessica was glad she had closed the far hatch; the equipment and maybe she herself might have been expelled through it. The segment of station in which she was standing, it was clear now, had been used as an airlock for the room beyond and the debris, as camouflage. In the next section someone had been living. A net-enclosed sleeping niche was in one corner and in another a closet that might house a toilet and perhaps a shower. A water spigot broke the smooth surface of a far wall next to plastic-fronted cupboards stacked with dehydrated food and quick meals, and a microwave.

The walls themselves were papered with posters and photographs. They were not of Earth but of space and astronomical objects—planets and stars and nebulae and galaxies, and artists' renderings of spaceships making their way among them.

Jessica felt a tap on the shoulder of her suit.

———

Jessica turned to face a person in another suit—but not the bearded man an over-active imagination had summoned. Features were not easy to discern in the helmet but she could see that the person had no beard. Then she recognized Cavendish. She started to switch on her suit radio, but Cavendish shook his head and motioned her forward. She pulled herself into the segment ahead and turned to see Cavendish follow. He swung himself around at the door and cycled it shut. After a few moments he eased his helmet loose, waited, and then pulled it off. He motioned Jessica to do the same.

Jessica winced at the odor in the room. Someone had been living there for a long time with little sanitation and less concern for cleanliness. Perhaps the waste-disposal system had malfunctioned. The place stank.

"What are you doing here?" she asked.

"I might ask you the same thing," Cavendish said. His left eye twitched.

"Someone's been living here," Jessica said.

"No doubt about that."

"It occurred to me maybe we were overlooking the obvious," Jessica said. "Maybe the sabotage came from the outside. We get so used to being alone up here; we don't consider other possibilities. Maybe those wild stories about the bearded man aren't just wild stories."

"So you came here to check up," Cavendish said. "It doesn't make any sense, though, does it? How could anyone avoid discovery when we were living in this place for a year before we dismantled most of it to build the ship?"

"No, it doesn't make any sense," Jessica said, "but here it is. Someone has been living here. Anyway, that's why I'm here. Why are you here?" She looked at Cavendish suspiciously. She had never fully accepted him and his place among them. She knew he had deciphered the original message, and that he had smuggled the information out of SETI and published it in the disguise of a UFO cult book; and she knew that his doubts about alien motives had driven him mad, or, rather, had reinforced his natural paranoia to the point of psychosis. But he was as responsible as anyone for gathering the crew that had built the ship and helping to persuade the Energy Board to allocate resources and let them go.

"I kept looking at the remains of the space station," Cavendish said, "and there was something wrong with it. I didn't know what it was until I began to compare its appearance with videos from the past. And then I realized—"

"What?" Jessica prompted, hoping it wasn't more of his paranoia. But then she remembered how her gaze had been drawn to the station time and again.

"That this part of the station was different. It wasn't here until a few months ago."

"That doesn't make sense," Jessica said. "Does it?"

"It makes more sense than the possibility that someone was living here and nobody noticed."

"Then you think—"

"That this is a space module designed to look like a part of the station, or a part of the station retrofitted to serve as a space module. It could have been an escape vessel in the original plans."

"You think it could have detached itself when we began arriving in orbit," Jessica said.

"And hidden itself god-knows-where. Maybe on the other side of the Earth. Maybe a few hundred kilometers away. We weren't looking for anything or anyone. We thought we were all alone."

"And then," Jessica said, "whoever it is decided to come back to see what we were up to. We can check it out. It should be easy enough to discover whether this section has jets and fuel tanks and controls. . . . But why did it return now, just as we are about to fuel the ship and test it?"

"Maybe you've just said why," Cavendish said.

"He—or she—but it must be a he. I can't imagine a woman putting up with this kind of filth," Jessica said. "He must want to stop us from going."

"That would fit in with the sabotage," Cavendish said.

"We've got to tell Adrian," Jessica said.

Cavendish shook his head.

"That's why you didn't want me to use the suit radio," Jessica said, "in case anybody was listening."

"If Adrian decides to postpone the fueling and the test run until we find out why this has happened and who is behind it, the saboteur will have succeeded," Cavendish said.

Jessica looked at him, trying to read his expression. All she could see was his left eye twitching. What he said made sense. It all fit together. And yet it was wrong. "We can't keep this to ourselves," she said. "That wouldn't be fair to Adrian or the crew or the mission."

"I think you're mistaken," Cavendish said. "Nothing must delay our project."

"But we don't know what other sabotage may already have been accomplished," Jessica said. "And we don't know where the person is who occupied this room."

Cavendish looked at the room with sudden surprise. Jessica followed his gaze. Someone had lived there, someone who worshipped space and the stars, a hermit who had brought his cave with him.

"Nothing must delay the project," Cavendish repeated, but this time his tone was different. He was pleading now, his eyes fixed on her as if his very existence depended on her answer.

"I don't agree," Jessica said. "But I'll wait until after the fuel is loaded."

Cavendish's eye twitched again, and Jessica wondered what she would do in this place isolated from everything and everyone if the unstable personality in front of her should snap. What if he attacked her to prevent her from doing what he clearly thought was against the best interests of the project, or his own? But she showed no signs of her unease. She put on her helmet and as she shoved herself forward, Cavendish moved aside and let her pass.

———

The antimatter was to be ferried from the nearest orbital converter by a vehicle shaped like an elongated dumbbell, with an engine on one end and a tiny pilot's saddle and controls on the other. In between, empty racks waited for vessels treated as gingerly as eggs and looking something like them—white and tapered toward the ends—or maybe more like oversized footballs for a game between Titans.

Alien devices shaped like giant moths were circling the sun, soaking up solar radiation, transforming it into high-energy gamma rays by means of alien-designed "magic crystals" constructed of "strange matter," and beaming them back to receivers in synchronous orbit. The receivers produced the antimatter from the gamma rays. One receiver had been diverted to storing its output in magnetic containers that Adrian, and a team of theoretical physicists and ingenious engineers, had constructed from the alien designs found in the appendices of Cavendish's book.

Would they work? Well, they—or devices similar to them—worked in orbit to store antimatter until it could be converted into energy beamed down to Earth. But vehicles had to ascend from the spaceship's near-Earth orbit to synchronous orbit, gingerly detach the magnetic vessels and place them with equal care into the clamps prepared for them, and bring them back to the ship's lower orbit. And there the vessels had to be removed and placed in new racks aboard the ship, fastened to devices that would allow them to be tapped, one by one, for their alien contents and fed, a small stream of ions at a time, into the magnetically shielded engine.

Jessica thought about all these things as she maneuvered the first ferry to dock with the receiver. A sleep period had passed since she had discovered the space-hermit's lair. Nights and days had no meaning in orbit, but for convenience most of the workers slept at the same time, with only monitors on duty. Jessica had not slept much, and when she had awakened she had avoided Adrian. It was easy to do in the bustle and suspense of fueling. Her skill in piloting and zero-gravity maneuvers was generally acknowledged, and she had volunteered. The thought that everything depended on her—everything they had dreamed and worked for—made her stomach churn, but the thought of *not* volunteering was even worse. And the thought of what her crewmates would think if she *didn't* volunteer.

The thought she finally settled on was that she would rather be handling the job than leaving it to someone less likely to pull it off without blowing up themselves and the ship, and maybe a few hundred thousand acres of home-world accidentally beneath at the moment of explosion. The orbital receiver was a maze of receptors and reflectors with an enigmatic spherical structure in the middle. The lethal eggs were racked outside the sphere where they had been deposited automatically once they had been filled with the most destructive substance in the universe.

She remembered what her mother had told her when she graduated from college and went out into the world on her own. "I have learned only two things in my life," her mother said, "and it's all I have to pass along to you." And then she said, "Nothing's easy" and "everything takes twice as long as it's supposed to." Her mother had been right more times than Jessica could remember, and now she would have looked at the business of transferring the antimatter containers and nodded. It wasn't easy and she suspected that it would take twice as long as it was supposed to.

As she flipped the switches that held the first magnetic bottle to the converter rack, she thought about Cavendish's aliens. She called them "Cavendish's aliens," because Peter's book had started it all. His cult book would have been considered a work of imagination, or psychosis, if anyone considered it at all, but Adrian had stumbled upon it and thought the designs might work. And they had. They had produced antimatter generators and a spaceship that might even prove capable of interstellar travel. And the spaceship might even take them to—what? Adventure? New worlds? The aliens who had sent the designs? Their hearts' desires?

Did Cavendish's aliens really exist, and if they existed would they be generous patrons distributing their largess to rational creatures wherever they existed? Or was there something dangerous, something explosive, at their core? Like the antimatter containers themselves, did they require delicate handling?

One by one Jessica brought the magnetic bottles to the ferry and snapped them gingerly into place until the broomstick was full. Then she maneuvered her cargo out of the converter maze into open space and waited until the spaceship arrived at a point when a slowing of her speed could lower her orbit to a near-Earth rendezvous. There she assisted with the unloading and storage of the eggs, fueled the ferry, and headed back to the converter. Not once but three times. Her mother was right. It took twice as long as it was supposed to, but, at last, the eggs were stored, she and the ship and the crew had survived, and the ship was ready for its test voyage.

Except for one thing. The crew. Who would go and who would stay behind? "Adrian wants to see you," Frances said as soon as Jessica removed her suit.

————

Adrian waited for her in the tiny conference room located between the living quarters and the control room. It doubled as a mess hall. Everything that wasn't a metal, load-bearing wall was made of lightweight plastic: tables, stools, clamps to hold trays and utensils, and vertical clamps for bottles. The room smelled of meals recently warmed in the microwaves that lined the walls, and over-riding that, of human effluvia that only registered when crewmembers came in from work outside.

But Cavendish was there, too, strapped onto a stool, looking paranoid and defiant at the same time.

Adrian studied her face. Jessica could feel him trying to gauge her trustworthiness.

"Why didn't you tell me?" he asked.

"What?"

"About the vehicle disguised as living quarters on the old station?"

"Peter argued that I shouldn't tell anyone," Jessica said forthrightly, "that it would only delay the test flight. I didn't like it, but I allowed myself to be persuaded. It looks like that was a mistake."

"Peter says it was the other way around, that you tried to persuade him."

"So I see," Jessica said. "If that's what he has told you, then one of us is lying. Either he talked me into not reporting it so that he could report it first and cast doubt on my loyalty to the project, which raises questions about his motivation, or I tried to conceal information that might be critical to its success. Who are you going to believe?"

Adrian steadied himself on the edge of the table to keep from floating away. "A difficult question. Peter has been involved in this project even before Frances and I—"

"And I was a Makepeace agent before I converted," Jessica said. "Maybe Makepeace planted me on the project. On the other hand, I've been a valuable member of the crew, and I've just retrieved and stored three loads of fuel." *And I'm tired as hell*, she could have added, *and my nerves are ready to snap from tension. And you've got me here answering foolish questions.*

Jessica had a foot hooked under a chair and didn't have to steady herself. She shook her head; the movement made her shoulders rotate.

"And Peter has been programming the computer," Adrian said. "It doesn't make any sense," he continued, postponing any decision. That was his major flaw. "There can't be any strangers among us, no bearded men, no ancient astronauts. Why should there be evidence of one?"

"There are stories—" Cavendish began.

"Space legends," Adrian said. "You get a bunch of people together under stress, and stories get started, myths get created and repeated until they lose their origins, people begin to believe in them."

"But the room—" Cavendish said.

"I've checked the computer records," Adrian said. "No astronaut is unaccounted for."

"Records can be doctored," Cavendish said darkly. "NASA wouldn't have wanted it known that they left an astronaut in orbit."

"No way they could have kept it secret," Adrian said.

"Then someone else has been living there," Jessica said.

"Peter said he followed you," Adrian said.

Jessica looked at Peter. Cavendish looked away.

"And he said you seemed to know where you were going."

"I had a hunch," Jessica said. "A sense of wrongness. If you saw it, you'd realize I couldn't live in such a mess. It would have to be someone who can sneak away without being noticed." She thought a moment. "Peter's assignment, programming the computer, leaves him unsupervised. He wouldn't be missed."

"And you've been working alone out on the hull," Adrian reminded her.

Jessica shook her head again. "The results of my seam checking are available on the computer. But if the room isn't evidence of a bearded astronaut left behind when the station was abandoned, someone else has been living there. Or it's a set-up."

"What do you mean?"

"Maybe it's a puzzle," Jessica said. "Put in place to slow us down. To give someone else time for—"

"What?" Adrian prompted.

"I don't know," Jessica said.

"It's not going to work," Adrian said. "We're going ahead on schedule."

"The test flight?"

Jessica saw Cavendish's body tense. At that moment she understood what was going on, but there was no way to prove it within the time available.

Adrian nodded. "The only decision we have to make is who is going with us."

————

A sleep-time later the entire crew, all awake at the same period for a change, scattered throughout the ship making last-minute checks of operations and systems that already had been checked many times before. Obsessive-compulsive behavior became normal, as the entire project, and the lives of those aboard, depended upon every part performing perfectly, except for the crew, whose inevitable mistakes had to be anticipated. And there were some alien-design functions built into the ship that Adrian and a few others thought they understood, but no one could be certain until the ship moved. That made everybody nervous, particularly Cavendish, who buried himself in computer readouts and simulations.

Finally, however, everything was declared as ready as it was likely to get, and Adrian assembled the crew in the largest of the three dormitories, the one for single men; the two smaller for single women and for couples. Contemporary mores mixed genders as if ignoring their differences could eliminate them, and the builders of the star ship expected growing fraternization. Eventually the largest dormitory might be turned over to the couples. But the designers—mostly Adrian—had decided that a certain amount of privacy, limited though it was by the spaceship volume and its necessary functions, would be a healthy preface.

Even the largest dormitory was crowded by the 212 people who had volunteered to construct the ship. One had been killed, one had been injured so seriously that she could not continue, and one had come down with multiple sclerosis. The conquest of space exacted casualties.

Some of the crewmembers sat on the edge of bunks, an arm or a leg wrapped around a tubular support. Others anchored themselves to the wall by the hand-holds placed at regular intervals, and others simply floated, at ease in free fall, in mid-air. Jessica was one of them.

Adrian was just inside the oval bulkhead, whose entrance could be sealed automatically in case of a meteor strike or other accident. Most of the construction crew could see him, but all could hear. "I don't have to tell you," he said, "that we are prepared to take a momentous step. Our job here is done, and our next challenge lies ahead. Not all of you signed on for that part of the adventure, and those of you who choose not to stay aboard for the test flight may wait in the remains of the old space station."

"I understand," he said, "that a new living facility has been added recently."

Jessica could feel Adrian's glance, but she was looking at Cavendish, clinging to the support of a nearby bunk. Cavendish was looking hard at Adrian as if forcing himself not to betray himself by looking at her. Then Jessica looked away to see Frances studying them both. Frances knew that Cavendish was avoiding looking at either of them. But Jessica wondered how much Frances knew and whom she believed. Adrian trusted Frances' judgment. Even though Frances reduced everything to familiar scenarios, she had been partnered with Adrian for twenty-five years, and they had brought this whole thing off, just the two of them. So what Frances believed counted.

Jessica thought back to her own beginnings. She had grown up secure and happy in a supportive California family, free to go where she wanted, to surfing or the tennis court or off to college, never doubting that she had a place to return to and people who loved her, no matter what, until the quake of '21 hit and her family was in the middle of it. The Energy Board could solve or ameliorate most human problems, but it couldn't control the natural processes of the Earth. Jessica never knew whether her family was killed when their house collapsed or by the tsunami that washed everything out to sea.

In the aftermath of that catastrophe, the recruiters for the Energy Board had looked like a new family, and she had reached out to them blindly. She had accepted one harmless assignment after another, mere bureaucratic information gathering, unaware that she had been identified by the agents working for William Makepeace. Even when she received the assignment of feigning an affiliation with a group of space enthusiasts, it seemed like only another way to gather information, and simulating a relationship with a man she had never met, and never heard of, seemed innocent enough. She was part of a family, and family did no wrong.

And then when she met Frances and later Adrian she discovered that life was not so simple. Life demanded choices between options that seemed equally attractive. Nobody knew how choices would turn out, so it was a matter of weighing facts and the logic that connected them. Ultimately, though, it boiled down to temperament: either you were conservative, like Makepeace, valuing what he possessed and what those around him possessed, which formed a seamless wall of covenants, and you were apprehensive of the change that might endanger those possessions; or you were adventurous, willing to try something new even if it cost you everything, enraptured by a dream and pursuing it past the point of pragmatic reality, hitching your wagon, literally, to a star.

That was why she had abandoned the family she knew for the dream she had only barely understood—that and the attraction of the man who owned the dream, or was owned by it, the unprepossessing Adrian Mast, whose soul was illuminated by his belief in humanity's future in space.

"So," he was saying, "we will test ourselves and our ship today. Nobody will hold it against anyone who wishes to leave. In fact, we will make it easy. There will be no guard on the exit hatch, and the monitors will be turned off. Those who choose to leave will be given an opportunity to rejoin the ship after the test run, or they may return to Earth on the next shuttle. Are there any questions?"

Cavendish looked as if he wanted to speak but remained silent.

"All right, then," Adrian said, "the test will begin in two hours. And may good fortune be with us on our maiden voyage."

Jessica looked at Frances and then at Adrian and finally at all the faces with whom she had grown familiar over the past few years. She realized that what she had chosen was a new family, but a family all the same, and the possibilities were great that this day she would lose this one, too—and life itself.

———

The engine started smoothly, almost imperceptibly. Louder than the whisper of the exhaust were the exhalations of breaths within the control room. Jessica hadn't realized until then that waiting for the moment of truth had been like waiting for the dentist's explorer to touch an exposed nerve or reaching the point on the roller coaster ride where it hesitates at its apex before plunging into space. She looked at Adrian, who was strapped into the pedestal chair next to her. He glanced at her and grinned. It was an expression at least as much of relief as joy.

Two other crewmembers in the control room monitored the engine-room gauges and the remote sensors, but otherwise it was Jessica and Adrian. Frances had complained of a headache and gone to the unmarried women's dormitory to lie down, but Jessica thought it was because she didn't wish to risk being space-sick in front of Adrian when the ship began to move.

Jessica looked at Adrian again. He nodded. She edged the ship out of orbit with the manual controls, careful not to approach the remains of the space station where members of the crew, as yet unspecified, had absented themselves, or to point the ship's exhaust in that direction. The antimatter should be completely annihilated in the magnetic-bottle reaction chamber, but no one knew if the design was perfect or if it had been perfectly translated into metal and strange metal. In the world where matter met antimatter, nothing less than perfection sufficed.

Jessica had not slept well the previous night. In fact, she did not remember sleeping at all. But now she felt alert, alive, exhilarated, as if she had set out to kill a dragon but had captured it instead and tamed it and rode it, wings flapping, into the sky. The ship that they had put together piece by piece and part by part, that had seemed as if it would never be complete or if complete would never function as intended, was an entity, by some gestalt magic turned into a living creature. Even the feeling of weight was different, pressing them into their seats, giving reality to what had seemed like airy insubstantiality.

The control room was silent as people concentrated upon their tasks, but a murmur came from the corridor. It was a sound like the well-bred approval of a Wimbledon point well-played, and Jessica realized that the crew, at stations throughout the ship, had broken into relieved conversation. "We're off to see the universe," she said to Adrian.

He nodded and grinned, as if he did not trust himself to speak.

As soon as the ship had cleared near-Earth orbit, Jessica accessed the next preprogrammed maneuver. Their velocity would gradually accelerate until the ship reached an orbit beyond that of the moon, which would be, by that time, on the other side of the Earth.

"I'm going to check on Frances," Jessica said.

"I should have thought of that," Adrian said.

Jessica made her way to the single women's dormitory, adjusting to the realignment of walls and floors under acceleration pressure. She missed the freedom of weightlessness, but that loss was balanced by the exhilaration of motion.

The dormitory was empty.

Jessica felt a flash of hope that Frances had, somehow, slipped away to join those who had absented themselves from this test run, but recognized the folly of that thought. Frances could not have left and would not have left, and Jessica did not want her to leave. The competition between them was nothing compared to their friendship.

Jessica found Frances in the single men's dormitory. She was standing in front of an open locker. Frances turned to look at Jessica as she entered. "I thought it was time to check on the absentees," Frances said.

"Adrian said—"

"Leaders can afford to be magnanimous only if they have skeptical lieutenants," Frances said. "We're launched on an adventure, and in every adventure scenario there's a weak character who is going to endanger everybody, and the quest itself."

"I always thought you had me picked for that role."

Frances shook her head. "That was always a possibility, but it's either the one you don't expect or the one you know is going to break, like Conway's brother in *Lost Horizon*. In this case, it was most likely to be someone who wasn't on the test flight."

"And how did you figure out who that was?"

"I turned the monitors back on. Nine people left the ship: Cavendish and eight of the people who were with him from the start, back at the abandoned Kennedy Space Center."

"Why am I not surprised?"

"That was clear after his accusation. The accuser is either unwisely ignored or is trying to shift suspicion from himself."

"Or trying to convince himself that his treachery belongs to someone else," Jessica said.

"That, too. But this pretty much clinches it," Frances said. She pulled an object from the open locker and held it, dangling, from her hand.

Jessica stared at it, trying to decipher what it was. Then it came into focus: it was a latex mask, like a man's skin slipped intact from his head. There was a bald head mottled with spots of age, a tanned and aged face, and a long, white beard....

"The bearded man," she said. "And the locker?"

"Peter's," Frances said.

From over the public address speakers Adrian's voice said, "I thought you'd all like to know: I've started the next programmed flight sequence."

Jessica knew what that meant. The ship was launched on a course for Mars. One of the tragedies of manned spaceflight was that the energy behind space exploration had dwindled before humanity had an opportunity to investigate any of the planets, even the nearer ones, and on their maiden test flight Adrian hoped to rekindle the popular imagination with a flyby.

The information about Cavendish may have come too late.

———

By the time Frances and Jessica reached the control room, plodding along in the traditional step-by-step that pleased Frances and annoyed Jessica, the ship had been accelerating for five minutes at a steady one gravity. The control room wasn't at all like those on the television shows Jessica had grown up with: it was sparse and utilitarian, with a semi-circle of pivoting armchairs mounted on pedestals and equipped with velcro belts. The chairs faced a curved, plastic counter top inset with dials and keyboards. Above that a series of vision screens showed the various working areas of the ship and exterior views in all directions.

No windows. Jessica recalled Adrian chuckling when Peter asked about the plans. "Windows!"

Jessica shook herself before she fell into one of Frances' genre pits. Identifying the genre wouldn't help this time.

Adrian swiveled around to face them, pleased with himself and his world. Jessica hated to spoil his mood. She looked at Frances.

"I found this in Peter's locker," Frances said, holding out the mask.

Adrian took in its meaning at a glance. "So," he said, suddenly sober, "Peter is the bearded man. I wonder what he hoped to gain by that. What does he have to say?"

"I don't think we'll ever know," Jessica said.

"He isn't around to ask," Frances added.

"That's a pretty fast search," Adrian said.

Frances shrugged. "He was among those who left." She seemed much more in control now that her trial by weightlessness was over. "You know the way things work. You propose and I dispose."

Adrian accepted Frances' breach of his word without comment. Jessica didn't know whether it was because he expected it or because they had more serious concerns. She hoped it was the latter. She didn't want to reevaluate the relationship between Adrian and Frances while she was still struggling with the implications of Frances' last sentence and Adrian's failure to react to it.

"That means we may be sitting on a time bomb," Adrian said.

"Clearly," Frances said.

"I feel sorry for Peter," Adrian said.

"I know."

Jessica looked from one to the other impatiently. "Why are you talk-ing about poor Peter when there's so much to done?"

"The question is," Adrian said, "what's to be done?"

"The ship is working like a dream," Frances said, "but there's no way of knowing when it will turn into a nightmare."

Jessica looked from Adrian to Frances and back again. "What are you saying? You don't even know what's wrong. You don't even know if any-thing is wrong." She moved impatiently to the pilot's chair and began looking at the readouts.

"If there's anything wrong," Adrian said, "—and there almost cer-tainly is something wrong—it will be in the computer. The glitch in the computer program two days ago was a test."

"And a warning we should have paid more attention to," Frances added.

Jessica hated the way Adrian and Frances completed each other's thoughts, like an old married couple. She typed in the command for the computer to switch to manual, but the ship continued its acceleration unaltered.

"We all knew how much this project meant to Peter," Adrian said. "It's still hard to believe that he would sabotage the only thing that would bring him peace."

"What we didn't know," Frances said, "was how great his fear still was."

Adrian shook his head, as if he was trying to clear it of clutter. "He started the whole thing. Without him there would be no alien message, no designs, no project."

"He stood in for humanity itself," Frances said. "Attracted by the mystery; afraid to find the answer. Attraction and repulsion. Balanced in most. Exaggerated in some, like Peter, to the point of anguish. Finally the fear got the better of him."

"We may well be in a difficult situation," Adrian said, "but it's Peter I feel sorry for. He'll never know. He has to know, and yet he never will."

"I hate to say this," Jessica said, "but that's the dumbest thing I've ever heard. Peter has been working for Makepeace. Only Makepeace could have arranged for the capsule that fit so neatly into what was left of the station, and only Makepeace could have come up with the scenar-io that landed us here. He doesn't want us to succeed. For earthbound humanity's reasons, sure, but most of all for Makepeace's reasons. I've worked for him and I know how he thinks."

Adrian and Frances exchanged glances.

"That may be true," Adrian said, "but it doesn't change anything."

"Well then, try this," Jessica said. "The manual controls don't work."

Adrian nodded. "And I'd guess there's nobody aboard who knows how to reprogram the computer."

———

Jessica looked at their eyes, first Adrian's and then Frances'. They were curiously unafraid. She realized that they were looking at her eyes, as well, and that in them they would read frustration and impatience and, yes, fear. She turned to the vision screens while she tried to gain control of her emotions. The rear view showed a rapidly retreating moon, and the one slightly to the side, a disappearing Earth still looking a fertile blue streaked with white. On the other side, where the sun would have been, the overload had closed down the receptors. Ahead was the star-strewn blackness of outer space.

She looked at the readouts. "We've been underway for an hour," she said calmly. "Our speed is thirty-five kilometers per second, and we're almost sixty-four thousand kilometers from Earth."

"If the program maintains this acceleration," Adrian said, "by tomorrow we'll be about one-sixth of the way to Mars."

Jessica input an inquiry. "Our course and speed has us arriving at Mars orbit two hours before the planet does. Unless something changes, it seems likely that Peter had something else in mind."

"And it seems likely," Frances said, "that if Peter had intended to destroy the ship, it would have exploded by now. Some celestial fireworks would have been a good object lesson for the rest of humanity."

"The question is," Adrian said, "what were Peter's intentions?"

"Jessica," Frances said, "you just got that information from the computer, didn't you?"

"Yes."

"You said it had locked you out?"

"I said it wouldn't let me change our acceleration or course, or switch to manual," Jessica said. "Everything else is proceeding normally. It's providing readouts, controlling air composition and temperature, showing us views, everything it was built to do—except letting us choose where we want to go and how fast. Like a virus that's taken over that one part of the computer."

"That means that Peter had some kind of plan."

"Like a one-way ticket to an unknown destination," Adrian said.

"I guess we'll know when we get there," Frances said.

"If he just didn't want to get rid of us with a ticket to nowhere," Jessica said.

Adrian shook his head. "That wasn't Peter's way. He had these twin compulsions of fight and flight. He couldn't bring himself to fight, but he couldn't bring himself not to seek the answers his neurosis needed. So he has sent us to find out the answers."

"Which he'll never know," Jessica said impatiently.

"Which he'll never know," Frances agreed. "And he'll grow old never knowing. He'll have psychotic episodes when he wants to kill himself because of guilt and others when he thinks he's getting messages from us or from his aliens. He's going to have a miserable existence and die a miserable death, wishing he were here, but at least he's going to know that we're out there, looking." Frances gestured toward the forward vision screen with its star-sprinkled vastness.

"It could be the aliens themselves," Jessica said. "It could be an alien virus, inserted who knows when, intended to bring us to them, like sheep to the slaughter."

"That sounds like Peter's paranoia," Adrian said.

"Or Makepeace's," Frances said.

"On the other hand," Adrian said, "Peter may well have had information that he was withholding."

"What kind of information?" Jessica asked.

"Information about where to go once the ship was built."

"Instructions from the aliens?" Jessica asked.

Adrian nodded.

"But why would he withhold it?" Jessica asked.

"Maybe he concealed it even from himself," Frances said. "Because it was too horrific."

"If it was too horrific for him, why shouldn't it be horrific for us?" Jessica asked.

"Because he's paranoid," Adrian said, "and we're not."

Jessica turned back to the keyboard at the pilot's station. "Maybe you're satisfied with going where Peter's paranoia takes you, but I'm going to learn how to master this computer. I'll break into its programs and make it take us where I want to go! After all, we've got all the time in the universe."

"And where do you want to go?" Adrian asked.

Jessica was silent for a moment. "I don't know. I just don't want to be—abducted." She swung back around to face them.

"Frances," Adrian said, "I think it's a good idea to develop the skills to reprogram the computer. Between Jessie and me, and whoever else has some talent for it, we ought to be able to figure out how to do that."

"That's a good idea," Frances said.

"But, Jessie," Adrian said, "once we do regain control, I think we'll have to consider leaving Peter's programming intact."

"But why——?" Jessica began.

"I think he programmed in the instructions about how to get to the aliens, the part of the original message he never revealed to anyone. And I think we won't ever find a more suitable goal, and we'll never be satisfied until we find the answers to our questions as well as Peter's."

"Why did they send us the plans?" Frances said. "What do they want from us? Who are they?"

Jessie turned back toward the vision screen that showed the depthless blackness littered with tiny lights that represented the long way ahead. Everything was orientation and a constant adjustment of one's relationship with the universe. If their acceleration remained constant, the ship would leave the Solar System in thirteen days and in another four hundred days or so they would pass beyond the Oort Cloud.

Behind them, looking at it from the viewpoint of the universe, would be cosmic debris. Ahead would be the abyss, the bottomless pit of interstellar space.

And even deeper, the mysteries of where they were going and what strangeness waited for them at the end of their voyage.

"Curiouser and curiouser!" cried Alice.

Lewis Carroll

⊨

Part Four

THE RABBIT HOLE

THEY EXISTED INSIDE AN EXPLOSION OF LIGHT. It filled their waking moments and their dreams. They heard it as a background of white noise; they smelled it underlying a stench of human and machine effluvia; they felt it like the warp of their world; they ate it with their breakfast cereal.

The external vision screens were blank. They had been turned off; nobody remembered who had done it or when. But they knew the glare was out there just beyond the walls of the ship. It was the only thing they knew for certain since they had entered the wormhole.

"No one knows what happens inside a wormhole," Adrian Mast said, turning in the swivel chair that faced the useless controls.

"Except us," Frances Farmstead replied.

They were inside the control room of the spaceship they had helped build. Although there was nothing to control, they found themselves meeting there as if by prearrangement. But that was impossible.

"If we really knew what was happening," Adrian said. "Or remembered from one encounter to the next."

"We should make notes."

"I've tried that," Adrian said. He wrote a note to himself on a pad of paper. He showed it to Frances. It read: *make notes*. "But I've never come across any record of anything I've written, on the computer or by hand."

"That's strange," Frances said, leaning back. "I'll have to try it."

"It's as if there is no before and after," Adrian said.

"It's a mystery," Frances said. She was seated in the swivel chair next to him. She was wearing loose-fitting khaki coveralls. Moments earlier, he thought, she had been wearing a kind of body stocking. No, that had been Jessica, and it wasn't moments earlier. It had been before they entered the wormhole.

"We've got to solve it like a mystery," Frances said. "Like Ellery Queen or Nero Wolfe. Putting together clues."

"There's something wrong with that," Adrian said, "but I can't remember what. Maybe that's the trouble. We can't remember."

"We should make notes," Frances said.

"I'll try that," Adrian said. "What's the last thing you remember?"

"We had been accelerating for a long time, and then—and then—"

The crew had built the ship from alien plans. But when they had started the ship on its first test run, the computer had implemented a program that sent them hurtling toward outer space.

They tried to reprogram the computer to take back control of the ship. But when they succeeded, they had to ask themselves: where else would they go? If they continued toward an alien-chosen destination they might find the answers to the other questions that had plagued them from the beginning: Why had the aliens sent the spaceship designs? What did they want from humans? What would humans find at the end of their journey, and what would happen when they arrived? If they arrived.

The ship had worked. Unlike most human designs, even though fallible humans had put the ship together, often from salvage, it worked the way machines and creatures in space had to work if they were to survive, that is, without a glitch. That nothing malfunctioned was due, as well, to Adrian's obsession with perfection, with his insistence on checking and rechecking everything. The ship had accelerated at one gravity past the orbits of Mars, of Jupiter, of Saturn, of Uranus, of Neptune, and finally of Pluto, and they had left the Solar System.

That took thirteen days. Moving beyond the Oort Cloud consumed another four hundred days. After a hundred days more of plunging into the abyss—a year-and-a-half of living in enforced proximity to two hundred other people, smelling their body odors, hearing their familiar anecdotes, speech patterns, and throat clearings, and eating recycled food—their tempers shortened and their anxieties grew. By that time Jessica Buhler had isolated Cavendish's program, and they had to fight the temptation to push the button that would put the ship back under their control and maybe cut them off forever from what had started them on this journey.

"I remember all that," Adrian said, rubbing his temples. "But what happened then?"

Behind them the sun had dwindled into just another star, and although the stars were everywhere all the time, they could not escape the feeling of being far from everything that mattered. Then the blankness of space opened a blazing eye and glared at them.

"It was like a white hole," Frances said, "suddenly in front of us...."

———

Conflicting gravities tugged at their bodies, as if all their loose parts wanted to go in different directions, as if their internal organs were changing places.... The glare was blinding. Jessica reached out with a hand that seemed to know what it was doing and slapped off the external vision screens. The relative darkness was blessed, but the wrenchings continued. If time had existed, the sensations would have seemed to go on forever, but then the twistings and displacements stopped as if they had never been.

The odor of fear filled the control room.

"I think we're in a wormhole," Adrian said, as if that explained everything.

"What's that?" Frances asked. She was seated in one of the chairs in front of a panel that had been useless for control since the ship began moving. Now its readouts were gyrating wildly.

"Some kind of distortion in space. Physicists have said they could exist, in theory, but nobody has ever seen one."

"What good is a wormhole?" Frances asked.

"It's supposed to take us somewhere else," Adrian said. "We entered one mouth; presumably there's another somewhere and the two are connected through hyperspace. Physicists thought they would look like black holes but without horizons."

"It looks more like a white hole," Frances said.

"Some scientists speculated that the relative motion of the wormhole mouths would boost the energy of the cosmic microwave background into visible light and create a kind of intense glare."

"Too bad they'll never know they were right," Jessica said. She was standing between Adrian and Frances with a hand on the back of each chair.

"These things, these wormholes, they're everywhere?" Frances said.

Adrian shook his head. "Natural wormholes ought to be small and ephemeral. This one was created."

"Why would somebody create a wormhole?" Frances asked. She didn't like anything that she couldn't connect with something that she had read or seen.

"To get from one part of the universe to another in a hurry. It may explain why Peter got a message in energetic cosmic rays. Sending a message over interstellar distances would have taken centuries, or millennia if the distances were really great. But if they were emitted from the end of the wormhole near the Solar System, the message would have arrived in little more than a year. And whoever is at the other end could have used it to know we were here, maybe even keep track of us."

"Surely they couldn't see anything from here," Jessica said. "Even the sun looked like just another star."

"They might be able to pick up energy transmissions, radio, television," Adrian said. "Maybe that's why they created it in the first place— because we started broadcasting back in the 1920s."

"This is so weird," Frances said. "Who could do something like this?"

"We couldn't," Adrian said. "Creatures far beyond our technical capabilities, maybe they could. What a physicist named Kip Thorne called 'an infinitely advanced civilization.' Damn! There's no 'maybe' about it. They did it, so they could do it."

"You said wormholes ought to be ephemeral," Jessica said. "This one seems to be persisting."

"So they not only had to create it," Adrian said, "they had to keep it from collapsing. Scientists think that would take something they call 'exotic matter,' something with negative average energy density, one of whose characteristics would be that it would push the wormhole walls apart rather than letting them collapse."

"Like antigravity," Jessica said.

"So what does it all mean?" Frances asked.

"We're inside something that doesn't belong to our reality," Jessica said, "and it is going to take us, if we're lucky, somewhere so far from Earth and our sun that we won't even be able to identify them in the night sky."

"And if we're not lucky?" Frances asked.

"We could spend our lives in here," Jessica said, "or have it collapse with us inside it, which might strand us in hyperspace, if we survived. I think that would be pretty bad."

"That's about it," Adrian said absently. He was looking at a pad of paper.

"What's wrong?" Frances asked. "Besides being lost."

Adrian showed them the pad. On it someone had written: *make notes.*
"Seems like a good idea," Frances said.

"Sure," Adrian said. "But I didn't write it. That is, I don't remember writing it. I remember that I will write it." He looked confused.

"I remember that," Frances said. Her voice was excited. "But it won't happen—"

"What's going on?" Jessica asked.

Adrian drew a square around the words on his notepad and then constructed a square on each side. "Space is different inside a wormhole. Maybe time is, too. Space and time are part of the same continuum. We may be in for some strange effects. At some point, for instance, I'm going to say, 'It's as if there is no before and after.' But that's wrong. The before may come after the after."

"Like remembering what hasn't happened yet?" Frances said as if she were making a joke.

"And maybe not remembering what has already happened," Jessica said.

"'It's a poor sort of memory,'" Frances said, "'that only works backward.'"

"Why does it sound like you're quoting from something?" Jessica asked. "Aside from the fact that you're always quoting from something."

"It's from *Alice in Wonderland*," Frances said. "Or rather from the sequel, *Through the Looking Glass*, and the reason it comes to mind is that, like Alice, we've fallen into a rabbit hole, and in Wonderland everything is topsy-turvy."

"I don't think we're going to find any answers in children's stories," Jessica said.

"I've always found Frances' fictional precedents helpful," Adrian said.

"The point is," Frances said, "that we're going to experience something that is likely to make us crazy unless we have something to cling to."

"Like what?" Jessica asked skeptically.

"When Alice fell down the rabbit hole, she encountered talking rabbits and caterpillars that smoked and cats that disappeared and who knows what all. Maybe we're going to run into the same sorts of things. If we can treat it like a kind of wonderland experience, meeting the strange but not surrendering to it, we can cope."

A patter of feet came from beyond the hatchway that led to the rest of the ship. Frances and Jessica looked at each other and then at Adrian.

"That sounded like children," Jessica said.

"'Curiouser and curiouser,'" Frances said.

———

In the middle of the night Adrian heard a rustling sound and something that sounded like a sigh. He pushed the switch beside his bunk, and overhead light flooded the tiny room. Jessica was standing just inside the open door, one arm out of the body stocking that was all she wore and the other arm halfway removed.

"What's going on?" Adrian asked, sitting up so suddenly the room spun around him.

"I didn't want to wake you," Jessica said.

"I mean, what are you doing in my room?"

Jessica looked around, as if the question that Adrian had asked was being processed. "I don't know. It seemed—natural," she said. "But now I can't remember why."

Adrian looked at the portions of Jessica's body that had been revealed: the smoothness of her skin and the curvature of what seemed, under most circumstances, athletic and slender. It was as if he were seeing her for the first time as a woman instead of a member of the crew.

"It's this damned wormhole," Jessica said, shrugging her arms back into the body stocking and closing the top with one stroke of her right hand.

But it wasn't the same as it had been before. Maybe it was because he had no imagination, Adrian thought, or maybe because his imagination was focused on distant goals, but now that he had seen Jessica as a woman it was difficult to see her as anything else. But he would, he knew; the wormhole would see to that.

"What's going on in here?" another voice asked from the doorway. It was Frances, solid and square in her pajamas, almost filling the space. The room was so small that she was standing next to Jessica.

"That's hard to say," Adrian replied.

Frances looked from Adrian to Jessica and back again. "Doesn't look that difficult to me. If this were a romantic film, the next scene would show lovers springing apart guiltily, or waking up together. If this were a suspense film, they would be plotting some kind of caper. If it were a mystery, one would be planning to kill the other."

"It's a farce," Adrian said.

"People wandering into each other's rooms without any reason and finding themselves in embarrassing circumstances," Jessica said.

None of this eased Frances' air of suspicion. "Oh, there's a reason. There's always a reason."

"You forget our wormhole inversions," Adrian said. He had his feet planted firmly on the deck.

"Whatever the problems we're having with cause and effect," Frances said, "a midnight meeting doesn't happen by accident." She frowned at Jessica as if they were in a contest and Jessica had broken the rules.

"I admit it looks suspicious," Jessica said, "but I wasn't trying to seduce Adrian."

Adrian flinched. The deck didn't seem so firm.

"It just seemed natural," Jessica said.

"Of course it did," Frances said.

"You know what I mean. Not something that was planned. God knows we can't do that inside this damned hole. Just something that seemed as if it had happened before."

"I'm not surprised," Frances said.

"If it did," Jessica said.

"And it didn't," Adrian said.

"You keep out of this," Frances and Jessica said almost simultaneously.

Adrian looked from one to the other. Frances started laughing. "You look like Cary Grant in *The Awful Truth*." Then her expression sobered. "We really need to come to an understanding."

"I know," Jessica said. "If we get out of this place, we're going to need children."

"They don't have to be his," Frances said. "There are lots of other men."

"We can't afford to waste any genetic material," Jessica said. "Chances are we'll never get back. Or if we get back, it may be in the remote past or the distant future. We may be all that's left of the human species. All of space-going humanity anyway."

"That's as it may be," Frances says. "But what's to say I couldn't have children?"

"No reason you couldn't," Jessica said. She put her arm around Frances' shoulder. "We've got doctors and we downloaded to our computers all the medical information available. Your uterus might not be up to the pregnancy bit, but your ova may well be harvestable."

"Thanks," Frances said. "But there's the emotion part."

Jessica hugged Frances harder. "We're going to have to get over that part. There's too much at stake."

Frances smiled and put her hand over Jessica's. "That's settled then. I'm glad we had this talk."

Jessica smiled back. "Me, too. I just wish we could remember it later."

Adrian looked from one to the other. "Wait a minute! What's going on here?"

"None of your business," Jessica and Frances said together.

"Come on, now," Adrian said, feeling confused and maybe frightened. "You're disposing of me like a prize cow—"

"Bull," Frances said.

"And you say it's none of my business?"

Frances reached over and patted Adrian's hand. "Don't worry! It will all work out. You take care of getting us out of here. We'll take care of the social arrangements."

Adrian looked from one woman to the other. "How are we going to get out of here?"

"You'll figure something out," Jessica said.

From outside the tiny captain's quarters came the sound of children's voices raised in some kind of game, but when Frances turned and Adrian reached the door, the corridor outside was empty.

———

When Adrian entered the control room, someone was seated in the chair that faced the prime computer station. That wasn't unusual—or at least it wouldn't have been unusual if the usual had existed as a comparison. What was unusual was that the head was familiar, and it should have been back in Earth orbit or, by now, back on Earth. But everything operated by different rules inside the wormhole, and the key to sanity was not trying to apply rules appropriate to normal existence. The person wasn't computing; it seemed to be reading a book.

"Peter," Adrian said. "What are you doing here?"

The chair turned. The person was Cavendish without a doubt, looking as real as Adrian, as solid as Adrian. "Same thing you're doing," Cavendish said. "Trying to find a way out of here."

"We left you back in Earth orbit," Adrian said reasonably.

"I remember that, too," Cavendish said. "Yet here I am."

"I don't think so," Adrian said. "I think you're some kind of illusion." He took a step toward Cavendish as if to confirm the existence of the other man by touching his shoulder.

"I wouldn't do that," Cavendish said.

"Why not?"

"If your hand passes through me, you're going to think your mind is going. If you find out I'm solid, that I'm really here, you're going to question your grasp on reality."

"You're the one who's supposed to be paranoid."

"And I'm not worried?" Cavendish shrugged. "Maybe that means I'm not really here. Or that what's here isn't really me."

Adrian went to the captain's chair, sat down, and swung around to face Cavendish. "Why are you here?"

"Things haven't worked out, have they?"

"That depends on what things you're talking about. The ship took us to this wormhole. That worked out. I gather that you programmed that into the computer."

"I just downloaded that part of the message."

"The part you didn't tell us about."

Cavendish shrugged. "It wasn't something I could share without creating crises of decision."

"So you made the decision for us."

"I didn't know that it would take the ship here. All I knew was that this was what the aliens wanted."

"They could have wanted to blow us up," Adrian said.

"If they didn't want us out here in spaceships, they wouldn't have sent the designs. It would have been a sorry joke to send the designs, with the antimatter technologies and everything, and have a few humans spend years building a ship just to destroy us."

"Then why didn't you come along?" Adrian asked.

Cavendish shivered. "You see? I am paranoid after all. I was afraid to go and afraid not to go. I was afraid not to have answers and afraid of the answers I might get. But I had to get some answers, even if only by proxy, and the only way any answers would emerge—although I would never know what they were—was by sending you to get them."

"Thanks," Adrian said.

"They were your answers, too," Cavendish said.

"Okay," Adrian said. "What hasn't worked out, then?"

"The wormhole. Passage should be instantaneous. But the ship is still inside."

"If we knew what 'still' meant. Time doesn't exist as we know it, in the wormhole. We've found that out, though it's hard to remember. So whatever is happening, in whatever order, or no order at all, may be happening in the instant we went into the wormhole and the following instant we emerge from it."

"On the other hand," Cavendish said, "this may be a test."

"What kind of test?"

"A test of sapience. Like we test rats in mazes. Maybe picking up the alien message was a test, and deciphering it was another, and getting to build the ship was a third, and building it so that it worked was another. This wormhole may be our maze, and if we don't do anything we may never get out."

"And if we get out," Adrian said, "what's our prize?"

"That's the big question, isn't it? That's what drove me into the protection of psychosis in the first place. Maybe the prize is a bit of cheese—or what cheese represents to a rat."

"More gifts like the antimatter technologies?"

"Or maybe aliens hungry for a different delicacy."

"Welcome to the galactic civilization?"

"Or insanity as we try to cope with the truly alien."

"Whatever it is," Adrian said, "we aren't going to know until we get out of here. Do we do nothing and hope that eternity comes to an end? Or do we do something—anything in the hope that it's the right thing?"

Cavendish looked uncertain and a bit fuzzy around the edges. "I don't think it would be a good idea to do anything until you have a good idea it will work."

"That's the trouble in here," Adrian said. "Not only is it difficult to make plans—it's difficult to figure out causes and effects, when the effects come first and the causes later."

"'Sentence first, verdict afterward,'" Cavendish said.

"You sound like Frances."

"There's a bit of Frances in me," Cavendish said. He was beginning to look transparent. "Just as there's a bit of you and of Jessica and maybe a tiny bit of me."

"I'd make a note of all this if I knew what you were talking about," Adrian said.

"And if you could find it after you wrote it."

"How do you know about that?" Adrian asked. He watched Cavendish's wispy form waver in the slight breeze from the air vents. Gradually the various parts of him began to disappear, first the feet and the hands, then the legs and the arms, and finally the torso, beginning at the hips.

"I'm not really here, you know," the ghost of Cavendish said. "You're really talking to yourself." His body had faded completely, and now only his head hung unsupported in the air.

"Some things you've said I didn't know," Adrian said.

"Nothing you haven't guessed or speculated about," Cavendish said. Now there was only a mouth. But it wasn't smiling. The corners were turned down in Cavendish's typical paranoid grimace.

Then he was gone. Adrian told himself that he would ask Frances what it all meant—if he could remember.

He looked down at the computer table. Cavendish had been reading *Gift from the Stars*.

———

The knock came on the door of the captain's cabin as Adrian was going over the computer readouts once more, searching for an answer that he would forget even if he found it. Adrian had not wanted to occupy the captain's cabin—more of a cubbyhole, really, like the ultra-compact quarters on a submarine. He preferred to bunk with the others in the single men's dormitory, leaving the only private accommodation on the ship for the privacy of conjugal visits, but the crew had insisted. Partly, he thought, out of their own sense of propriety.

"Come in," he said, putting the book he was reading on the surface that passed for a desk when it was pulled down, and turning on the stool that passed for a desk chair when it was not folded into the wall.

The airtight door slid aside. Jessica was standing in the narrow corridor, fidgeting from one foot to the other, looking concerned. That was nothing different. They all were.

"Do you have a moment?" Jessica asked.

Adrian gestured at the readout. "That's all any of us have."

Jessica sidled into the room and sat on the edge of the bunk. Her knees were only a few inches from Adrian's and that was uncomfortably close. "We've got a problem."

"I know. Not only are we in a reality where the normal rules don't apply, where even the laws of physics seem to be different, we can't make plans because we don't remember anything from one series of related events to the next."

"As long as events have some continuity," Jessica said, "they seem to hang together, pretty much, one following the other in before-and-after sequence. It's when the continuity is broken that causality is suspended."

"Or reversed," Adrian said. "We do remember things that haven't happened yet. So maybe what we have to do is to lay the groundwork for what we will remember earlier. At that point, maybe, we will know what to do and be able to do it."

"Which, of course, would get us out of this place before we had a chance to lay the groundwork necessary for the proper decision."

Jessica was sharp and a hard worker—in fact, she was his most reliable assistant. He knew this voyage would never have started without her, and it was likely that it wouldn't continue without her either. "I know," he said. "It's crazy. But what we have to remember is that what makes sense is probably worthless and only the right kind of nonsense will work."

She leaned forward to put a hand on his knee. "But that isn't why I'm here."

Adrian shivered. It wasn't that he didn't like to be touched. Frances put her arm around his shoulder and hugged him. Other crewmembers patted him on the back and shook his hand. This was different. He didn't want to think about what made it different.

"We haven't had any time for personal matters," Jessica said. "We've been too busy with building the ship. Now we've got nothing but time until we find a way to get out of the wormhole."

"Yes, time," Adrian said. He couldn't think of anything else, anything that would stave off what he feared was coming. He could make decisions about life and death but he wasn't good at what came between.

"We're a band of humans split off from the rest of the species, and there's little chance we'll ever get back."

Adrian nodded.

"So," Jessica said, "we've got to think about survival."

"That's all I think about."

"Not just us. The little band. What we stand for. The human species in space."

Adrian cleared his throat. The room was getting stuffy. "Yes?"

"We must make arrangements."

"Arrangements," Adrian said.

"We've got to pair off. We need to think about having babies and the gene pool and everything else."

"Everything," Adrian repeated.

"I know you don't like to talk about things like this, or think about them either," Jessica said. "So we women have to think about it for you, make plans, arrange things."

"You mean you've discussed this?" Adrian said huskily. "You and the other women?" He realized that he sounded incredulous, but he couldn't help himself.

"Of course not," Jessica said. "But we know. And I wanted you to know that I've always admired you, as a leader and as a man. Not only that, I like you." She leaned forward and kissed him.

For a moment, surprised, he responded. Her lips felt soft and sensual. Then he drew away, shocked at the way his body had responded.

Jessica stood up. Suddenly he was aware of the fact that underneath the one-piece garment she was wearing, only a foot from his face, was the body of a woman, and it was the body of a desirable woman, and if he understood what was going on it was his if he wanted it.

"I'm glad that's settled," she said, leaned down to kiss him on the cheek, and went through the doorway and down the hall.

"Settled?" he said, too late to be heard. "Settled?" He had one saving thought: at least all this would be forgotten like everything else.

He thought he heard laughter somewhere down the hall, but it came from voices he had never heard before.

―――

Adrian wasn't good at talking to groups, but Frances had said it was necessary and he knew that was true. He would have been as traumatized as the crew if he had experienced over the past few hours the time reversals and the gravity wrenchings of the wormhole transition, even though they had been forgotten, and was depending on someone else to solve the problems. Adrian was as puzzled about what was going on as the crew, but he was in charge. That meant whatever was done would be done by him, and, moreover, he couldn't appear to the crew the way he really felt—helpless.

He had gathered the crew twice before, the first time before the test flight, when he had offered the opportunity to depart, unobserved, to anyone who wanted to sit out the test flight. The second meeting had discussed the computer program that was guiding the ship out of the Solar System, and the reasons for allowing the course to continue toward what they assumed to be an alien-selected destination.

After that the crew divided itself into groups—work groups and social groups, which were not always the same. The crew had been assembled from volunteers to build a ship; once that was done it had to discover new skills and new interests. At first that shakedown was enough to fill the hours. Later squabbles arose about social arrangements and romantic pairings that had to be settled by counseling from Frances or, failing that, a ship's court, and if that was not acceptable an appeal to the Captain's final review. Now, however, he had to face them all and explain the inexplicable.

They were gathered in the couples' dormitory, which had been the single men's dormitory before the inevitable pairings had led to the switch. As in the two times before, men and women were seated on bunks or stools, or stood wherever they could see Adrian. Frances stood behind Adrian and to his left, providing the support of her solid presence. Jessica, on the other hand, stood by the door as if guarding the avenue of their escape. The climate in the room had been transformed from the intense boredom of spaceflight broken periodically by personal successes, disappointments, and disputes to a communal unease broken by moments of panic.

"We knew we would encounter some strange phenomena out here," Adrian said. "But we didn't know it would be this strange!" The crew responded with nervous chuckles.

"We have been through an experience that defies explanation," Adrian continued. "It is connected to our entering a wormhole. We know that much. We must have felt some gravity fluctuations."

"Why do you say 'must have'?" a man's voice asked from several bunks back.

"That's what we would expect from a wormhole, George," Adrian said, "but we're still here, so we survived them. If you're like us, however, you don't remember."

"I don't remember anything that happened after we entered whatever it was," another man said. "And that scares me!"

"It's enough to scare anybody, Kevin," Adrian said.

"There's something else," a woman said. "I'm remembering things that never happened, like an argument Bill and I had—are going to have."

"And I remember the way we are going to make up," a man answered. He laughed as if he were pleased with himself.

"We've got a theory about that," Adrian said. "You're remembering things that haven't happened yet, because time is mixed up in here. But we can't let the unusual get to us if we're going to figure out what's going on, and get out of this place."

"When's that going to be?" a woman asked.

"We don't know a lot, yet, Sally," Adrian said, "but we know this much: 'when' is a word that doesn't mean much where we are. A wormhole is an out-of-this-world means of getting from one place in the universe to another, like folding space so that distant points touch, and crossing there. The wormhole exists in some kind of hyperspace where space and time get mixed up. We think—"

"Why do you keeping saying, 'we think'?" a woman asked nervously.

"This is all new and different for us as well as you, Joan," Adrian said. "Give us a chance to figure this out, how this new kind of time operates and how we can function within it, and, I assure you, we'll get out of here and on our way."

Frances spoke up. "You might think about *Alice in Wonderland* and *Through the Looking Glass*. Alice was in a place where nothing made sense, but she stayed calm and eventually she got back to her safe, sane home."

"This ain't a children's book!" a man said. "And this ain't fiction."

"Sam, I hope we can be as capable of handling the unknown as a Victorian child," Frances said. "Maybe even get some answers."

"We ain't never going to get back, are we?" a woman said.

"We can't be sure of that yet, Lui," Adrian said.

Jessica spoke up for the first time. "But we've got to behave as if that's true, or we've got no chance at all."

"What I want to know," a woman said, "is where 'on our way' is going to take us."

"We don't know, Yasmine," Adrian said. "But we all signed on to have our questions answered, and we're going to have to follow the yellow brick road wherever it leads us until we get the answers."

A man said, "What's 'the yellow brick road'?"

Adrian smiled. "Frances has me doing it now."

"That's another children's book," Frances said.

"I'd rather come up with my own answers," another man said.

"If you come up with any, let me know," Adrian said. He folded his arms across his chest. "Meanwhile, we're going to have to live with uncertainty and forgetfulness and not let it make us crazy. But there's a way out of here. The wormhole was a confirmation that we are headed in the right direction. What we can be sure of is that we weren't directed here simply to strand us in Wonderland. This is a pathway. We just have to figure out how to move along it."

"Moving along it reminds me," Frances said, "of what the chess queen said to Alice in *Through the Looking Glass*: 'Now here, you see, it takes all the running you can do, to keep in the same place. If you want to get to somewhere else, you must run at least twice as fast as that.'"

"What's the good of that?" a man asked gruffly.

"We don't know, do we, Fred?" Frances said. "But I have a memory that it's going to matter. Oh, dear! That doesn't make sense, does it?"

"Frances, you're always finding a moral somewhere," a woman said.

"'Everything's got a moral, if you can only find it,'" Frances quoted triumphantly.

Shortly after that the meeting ended, with the crew informed but not relieved. For the moment, at least, they were not rebellious. Adrian had an uneasy feeling, however, that something about the meeting wasn't right: the room was more crowded than it had ever been before.

But he promptly forgot.

———

Adrian was alone in the control room when the deputation arrived. Three were men; two were women. All of them were young and all about the same age, late teens, maybe, or early twenties. In their youth and energy, they all looked a lot alike. One of the men and one of the women were blond; two of the men were dark-haired and one of them was dark-skinned; the second woman had dark hair. Adrian had never seen them before.

The dark-haired woman reminded Adrian of Jessica. One of the men looked familiar, too, but Adrian couldn't quite decide whom he looked like.

"We're here to present our demands," that young man said. His voice sounded familiar, too.

Adrian tried to keep from flinching. "Who are you?" he asked.

"You know who we are," the blond girl said.

Adrian shook his head. "You're all strangers. And the strangest part is that we're in a wormhole inside a ship that nobody can leave or enter."

"We're the next generation," the woman said.

Adrian was seated in the captain's chair. The five newcomers formed a semi-circle around him, lithe, athletic, and leaning slightly forward as if they were poised to take him apart. "We've been here that long?" Adrian asked.

"Duration is a word that has no meaning," the first young man said.

"It's hard to break old habits," Adrian said.

"We don't have any to break," the other dark-haired young man said. He sounded bitter.

"We agreed to keep this civil," the first young man said. He looked back toward Adrian. "We're here to present our demands."

"You've got to let me get used to the idea that the crew has had children who have grown up while we have been stranded in a wormhole that was supposed to provide instantaneous passage. I don't feel twenty years older."

"That's old-fashioned thinking!" the blond young man said contemptuously.

"He can't help it," said the young man who appeared to be the spokesman for the group, if not, indeed, its leader. "He's system-bound."

"He's got to help it," the blond young man said. "He's the captain."

"How many of you are there?" Adrian asked.

"Many," the blond young woman said.

"Enumeration is as difficult as duration," said the spokesman.

"Are you all the same age?" Adrian asked.

"You see?" the young man asked. "He'll never learn."

"Sometimes yes, sometimes no," the spokesman said patiently. "None of these questions you're asking has any meaning unless we get into normal space. And that's what we've come about."

"To present our demands," the blond young woman said.

Adrian folded his hands across his lap. "I don't know what you can ask for that we can provide, but go ahead."

"We want you to stop trying to get out of the wormhole," the spokesman said.

"We can't do that!" Adrian said.

"Why not?" the young man said.

"We're in never-never land," Adrian said. "Nowhere. No memory. No continuity. Virtual non-existence. And then, you see, we committed ourselves to finding out why the aliens sent us the plans for this ship and brought us here." He gestured at the book lying in front of him; it was *Gift from the Stars*. Often he found himself reading it as if he could find therein a way out.

"We didn't," the bitter young man said.

"Didn't what?" Adrian asked.

"Sign up for this trip."

"But—" Adrian began.

"You've got no right," the spokesman said, "to take us somewhere against our will."

"And against our right to exist," the dark-haired young woman said.

"What's that?" Adrian asked.

"What do you think will happen to us if you get out of this wormhole?" the spokesman asked.

Adrian was silent.

"We won't exist."

"What kind of existence is that?" Adrian asked finally. "What is life without memory? What is existence without cause and effect?"

"The only kind we know," the bitter young man said.

"We are your children," the spokesman said. "You brought us into this world, crazy as it seems to you. But it's our world, and you owe us."

"He also owes the rest of us," a woman said from the door. It was Frances. "And the species. If you're more than illusions, you'll be born at the right time in the right place. But now—be gone. You're nothing but a pack of possibilities."

The five turned toward her, frightened and uncertain, and disappeared like snowflakes evaporating before they hit the ground, leaving their potentials etched into the air.

Adrian rubbed his forehead. "They were so—real. So like the children the crew might have had—might have. Our language wasn't meant for in here."

"One of them looked like Jessica," Frances said.

"And another one—" Adrian began and stopped.

"What?"

Adrian looked into one of the darkened vision screens. There were no mirrors in the control room, but he could see his reflection. He knew who the spokesman for the group looked like.

He looked like Adrian.

———

A familiar figure with a familiar walk and a familiar look to the back of his head turned at the far end of the corridor and, before Adrian could speak, disappeared down the side corridor that led toward the mess hall. It was a man. Adrian was sure of that. "Hey!" he called out, but by the time he reached the corridor it was empty. Only Frances was in the mess hall, cleaning the table that doubled for conferences, and she looked puzzled when he asked if anyone had just come in or passed.

But when Adrian returned to the corridor leading back toward the control room, he saw the same figure in front of him. He ran toward it, but it got farther away the faster he ran. By the time he got to the control room, it was empty. He went back down the corridor, trying to figure out what it meant. When he turned to look behind, he saw the back of the figure again, still moving away. This time Adrian turned and went the other direction, and came face to face with the man just outside the mess hall.

"Adrian!" they each said. Then, "I don't believe it!"

"We'd better speak one at a time," Adrian said.

"I agree," Adrian said.

"We've got to decide, first, who's the real Adrian and who is the doppelganger," Adrian said.

"I'm real," they said together.

"Look," Adrian said, "this isn't getting us anywhere. I'll tell you what. As Frances would say, '"if you believe in me, I'll believe in you."'

"That sounds reasonable," Adrian said. "Maybe this is the opportunity we've been looking for—to find a way out of this place. Let's go in here and talk about it."

Adrian nodded. "We can put our heads together."

And Adrian added, "Two heads are better than one."

When they entered the tiny mess hall, Frances was gone. Adrian didn't think enough time had passed for Frances to have completed her clean up and departed. He didn't know whether that meant he was in his doppelganger's reality or whether it was another example of the wormhole's vagaries.

"Obviously," Adrian said, seating himself on a stool at the table, "the time variables have us tied up."

"Obviously," Adrian said, leaning back against one of the microwaves, not wanting to put himself in a mirror-image position. "But what isn't obvious is what we're going to do about the fact that we only remember what happens later."

"That's true," Adrian said. "So the secret is to prepare later for what we need to know earlier."

Adrian nodded. "I've thought of that. At least I think I've thought of that. The difficult part is remembering that we have to store information for earlier use."

"We have to come to that realization independently, every time. We have to learn to think differently, just as we have to learn to think differently about Jessica and Frances."

"What do you mean?" Adrian asked.

"It's clear to me, and it should be clear to you, that both Jessica and Frances are fond of us."

"And I'm fond of them," Adrian said.

"One is, or maybe both are, going to want that relationship to get even closer."

Adrian nodded. "That's an uncomfortable thought, but if it happens I will have to handle it."

"When we 'handle it,' as you say, we will have to think in unaccustomed ways."

"I know," Adrian said.

"I don't mean just the business of allowing emotional involvement, even intimacy, but the possibility of sharing, or being shared."

Adrian took a deep breath. "I understand you. What am I saying? I am you."

"In the same way," Adrian said, "we are going to have to think about our physical predicament in unconventional ways. Logic doesn't work."

"We'll have to try illogic," Adrian said. "As a matter of fact, I've already tried it. I caught up with you by going the other way."

"I was the one who caught up with you," Adrian said and then waved his hand. "No matter. We'll have to think impossible things."

"As Frances would say, 'I can't believe impossible things.'"

"I daresay you haven't had much practice," Adrian continued. "When I was your age, I always did it for half an hour a day. Why, sometimes I've believed as many as six impossible things before breakfast."

Adrian moved from in front of the microwaves. "I'm glad we had this meeting, even though it was a bit of a shock." He didn't offer to shake hands with the other Adrian. That would have been too much. "But I hope it doesn't happen again."

He went through the doorway into the corridor. This time he didn't look back.

————

They all knew it was time to act. Jessica looked at Adrian, Adrian looked at Frances, Frances looked at Jessica. They had been in the wormhole too long. None of them knew how long it had been: days, weeks, maybe even years. But they knew that if they didn't do something soon they would never get out.

Jessica looked at the gyrating readouts on the control panel. "We have to know what is going on outside," she said.

"None of our instruments work," Adrian said. "Or if they work, they aren't recording."

"We could turn on the vision screens," Frances said.

Jessica turned them on. The glare was blinding. "I think we've tried that before," she said. She turned them off.

"That's the cosmic microwave background boosted into visible light," Adrian said.

"I think the vision screens are as unreliable as the readouts," Jessica said. "We try to cut back on the light, and the screens go black. Somebody has to go outside and report."

Adrian nodded. "I agree. And I'm the only one who is capable of making sense of what is happening. I'll get ready."

"You can't be spared," Frances said. Her face had that "there's-no-use-arguing-with-me" look.

"Frances is right," Jessica said. "I'm the most experienced in working on the outside, the youngest, the most athletic, the steadiest—"

"You can't be spared either," Frances said. "You're young, all right, and you have a life ahead of you if we ever get to a place where you can live it. That leaves me."

"There's radiation out there," Adrian said. "God knows what. Even if it isn't fatal, whoever goes out there is going to take a lot of damage."

"Besides," Jessica said, "you get sick just turning your head quickly."

"I can do this," Frances said. "I can do whatever I have to do. And you've got a young body and young ova—all that needs to be preserved if we're going to have a future." She stood in front of them both, in the control room, square and ready.

"I'm not going to talk you out of this, am I?" Jessica asked.

Frances shook her head. "In a movie you'd hit me on the head and take my place, but this isn't a movie and it isn't going to happen."

"I'm glad you know the difference," Adrian said. "No heroism."

"Just common sense," Frances said. "Now I need some help in getting into a suit." She smiled at her admission of inadequacy.

Spacesuits had not been built for someone as short and wide as Frances, but a man's suit had been adapted by removing sections of the leg and welding the remaining pieces together. That didn't help Frances' agility, but then she hadn't used the suit much. Now she struggled into it, and Jessica checked all the closures twice.

"Don't stay out there more than a minute or two," Jessica said, "and don't try to do more than a simple survey. Be sure to snap yourself to the interior hook and make certain your magnet is firmly attached to the outer hull before you—"

"Hush," Frances said. "You're only making me nervous."

She turned and hit the large button beside the inner hatch. It cycled open as Frances turned, patted Jessica's shoulder with her glove, and touched Adrian's hand. She adjusted her helmet and stepped over the sill into the airlock.

Jessica spoke into her handheld microphone. "Can you hear me? Be sure you keep your mike open all the time. I'm going to suit up so that I can come out and get you if you're in trouble."

Frances shook her head inside the helmet as she pushed the inner button and the door began to close. "We don't want to lose two of us," she said. "Don't worry. If I don't get back, it's been a great run." But her face looked pale before the door completely closed. "I'm opening the outer hatch. God, it's bright out here!"

Jessica looked at Adrian, and Adrian looked back, but their thoughts were outside. "What's going on?" Adrian asked.

"I'm darkening my face plate. There, that's better."

"What can you see?" Jessica asked.

"Wait a minute. I feel a little sick. There's nothing to look at."

"Frances!" Jessica said. "Look at the airlock. Look down at your feet. Then look at the ship. Orient yourself to the ship!"

"Got it!" Frances said. "The ship seems to be moving. I can see some kind of disturbance in the glare that might be exhaust, so the engine is still operating, but we knew that, since we've had gravity."

"Which way are we going?" Adrian asked.

"Hard to say," Frances said. "There seems to be a dark place in the glare."

"Which direction?" Adrian asked.

"Toward the rear of the ship," Frances said triumphantly. "Where the antimatter stuff comes out."

"That must be the mouth of the wormhole where we entered," Adrian said.

"That's enough," Jessica said. "Come in."

"Not yet," Frances said. "I'm looking around while I'm here."

"Don't look around!" Jessica said.

"Funny stuff out here," Frances said. "A weird-looking contraption just went by. All twisted pipes and girders. Speaking of ships that pass in the night!"

"You're not doing us any good out there," Adrian said.

"There's another ship, or vehicle, or something," Frances said. "Only it's like a stack of waffles with a flagpole through the middle."

"Frances!" Jessica said. "You're making us nervous."

"Goodness knows, you've made me nervous often enough," Frances said. "There's an alien, I think. A creature of some sort with tentacles. And one shaped like a cone with eyes. And another, and another!"

"You're losing touch!" Adrian said. "Come back! Now!"

"There's the Mad Hatter!" Frances shouted. "And Humpty Dumpty. And the caterpillar smoking the water pipe. And the Queen!"

"Come back!" Jessica said softly. "Come back, Frances!"

"Off with their heads!" Frances said.

Adrian looked at Jessica. She turned and began climbing into her spacesuit.

"Remember," Frances said. "You have to run twice as fast as that!"

Something clanged from outside the ship, like a magnet being freed and metal-shod feet pushing against the hull.

Jessica stopped halfway into her suit. "I knew I should have gone," she said.

Adrian shook his head. "There's no way we can go faster," he said. "But maybe we can make Frances' sacrifice meaningful." He didn't know how that was going to happen, but, as unshed tears burned his eyes, he knew he would make it happen.

———

Jessica slapped the vision screens back on and let the glare fill the control room. "We've got to do something. Frances has—is going to—oh, I don't know what the right tense is. But she has given us all the information we're likely to get, and she's dead—surely she's dead."

"There's not much doubt about that," Adrian said. "We're remembering things that have yet to happen, including things that might happen, and we've got all the memories of what has yet to happen that we're likely ever to get."

"Even though we've just entered the wormhole," Jessica said.

Adrian nodded. "That's the funny way time works in here. Now we know but later on we'll forget. So we've got to do it now."

"Frances said we had to run twice as fast," Jessica said.

"And I said there was no way to do that," Adrian said, "or any reason to think going twice as fast would get us anywhere." He looked around at the control room. In spite of the glare, for the first time he was seeing things clearly—Frances, Jessica, the aliens and their plans. "We've been trying to reconcile the irreconcilables, the time anomalies, our own inability to adjust to inversions and potentials."

Jessica looked at him hopefully, the way an apprentice looked at her master, anticipating wisdom.

"We've got to turn the ship around," Adrian said. He turned to the controls. "Go back the way we came. If we were in real space, we'd have to decelerate for as long as we've accelerated, but this is hyperspace and we haven't moved far from where we entered."

"Let me do it," Jessica said. She began punching instructions into the computer. "But isn't that just giving up?"

"Maybe," Adrian said. He tried to isolate a cold feeling in the pit of his stomach. Maybe it was giving up. "Logically we should come out the way we came in, and then everything will have been for nothing—all our psychological torment, the felt years of experience, Frances' sacrifice—"

"But maybe not?" Jessica said.

Adrian could feel the ship swinging even though there was nothing to see, no way to get information from gauges, nothing but glare....

Something surged.

Conflicting gravities tugged at their bodies, as if all their loose parts wanted to go in different directions, as if their internal organs were changing places. Then the glare and the gravity fluctuations stopped suddenly. Adrian and Jessica looked at each other, remembering everything that had happened or might have happened inside the wormhole. They turned to look at the vision screens. The glare was gone. Outside was the blackness of space with here and there the pinpoint hole of a star. It could have been anywhere in the galaxy, including back near the spot from which they had been drawn into the wormhole.

Jessica adjusted the controls and new arenas of space swam into view. The stars were few and distant. A single star loomed closest, but it was old and faint.

"That isn't our solar system," Jessica said. "That isn't our sun."

Adrian shook his head. "Wherever we were going, we've arrived."

"How did you figure it out?" Jessica asked.

"If time was inverted," Adrian said, "maybe space was, too. In order to get out, we had to reverse our course. But then, I had some help." He thought about the other Adrian, who now would never exist, except maybe in the never-never world of the wormhole, and how he had caught up with him only when he went the other way. But maybe that never-never existence, like that of the children and maybe even of Cavendish, was as real as any other. "Maybe I'll tell you some time."

"Meanwhile," he continued, "I think we have managed our rite of passage and have a rendezvous with destiny."

"Whatever that means," Jessica said.

Adrian smiled at her. There would be great moments ahead, he thought, and moments of tenderness and fulfillment and maybe distress and regret and pain. But it would be living.

He heard a noise behind him and turned toward the entrance.

"Frances?" he said. "Frances?"

For who would lose,
Though full of pain, this intellectual being,
These thoughts that wander through eternity,
To perish rather, swallow'd up and lost
In the wide womb of uncreated night,
Devoid of sense and motion?

JOHN MILTON, *Paradise Lost*

⊢⊣

Part Five

UNCREATED NIGHT

THE IMAGE IN THE VISION SCREENS frightened Frances in ways she could not identify.

The small K-type star hung against the backdrop of empty space like a lantern set out for the weary traveler. Beyond loomed the impenetrable night of the intergalactic void. Behind glowed the remote swarm of what Adrian thought was the Milky Way galaxy. In front of the spaceship from Earth waited the goal of their long journey, this odd single planet, a bit larger than Mars but smaller than Earth, in an eccentric orbit around an old sun, here at stars' end.

The battered spaceship had been making its way toward the strange system for six months at one-gravity acceleration and six months more at one-gravity deceleration. A year of travel after their emergence from the wormhole that had spit them out on the far edge of what might be still the local galaxy. "But it could be any galaxy, couldn't it?" Frances asked. "What's distance to a wormhole? If it's like jumping across a folded sheet of paper, one place is as close as any other."

Frances stood behind Adrian and Jessica. They were seated in the control room of the ship they had decided to call *Ad Astra* but Frances insisted on referring to as *Aspera*—since she had suffered from space sickness and other problems during the trip. The control room provided evidence of long occupation: the air was thick with humidity and the odors of imperfect human bodies and not-quite-perfect machines, paint was worn down to bare metal in places, panels were dented, gauges flickered or were dark. But the vision screens were clear, and what they revealed was disturbing.

"True," Adrian said, "but it's difficult enough to keep track of intelligent life in one galaxy. Why cross intergalactic space? What could be the purpose of that?"

"What could be the purpose of sending spaceship plans across the galaxy and building a wormhole to bring us here?" Jessica asked.

That question had propelled them and their crew across measureless space and across twenty-five years from its obscure beginning. And a disorienting few hours—or many subjective years—in the wormhole had brought them to the place where they could see their journey's destination. But they still had no answers to the question of why the aliens had sent them the plans, what the aliens wanted from humanity—or any other creature who might receive those cosmic rays and have the scientific understanding to record them and the wit to decipher them and the technology to turn them into a vessel capable of traversing space. Did they want to help humanity, or themselves? Were they benefactors or predators, or simply disinterested observers? These were the questions that had toppled the original genius, Peter Cavendish, over the precipice edge of sanity into the chasm of madness.

And now they were close to their destination and maybe to their answers. The little world they were approaching seemed to be studded with objects like cloves in a Christmas orange. When they got near enough they realized the studs were spaceships like their own. Or maybe not quite like their own, and maybe only the starting point for new questions. Like: what were all those other strange ships doing in orbit around the little planet? It was like a Sargasso of space. They had thought the message was a summons just to them, but maybe the invitation had been broadcast to the universe and they were only the last to respond....

————

Within a few hundred kilometers from the world—if that was what it was—Adrian and his fellow travelers could make out finer detail on the vision screens of the control cabin. The ships were of many sizes and shapes and colors, as if the only thing they had in common was that they could traverse space. Some of the colors were so strange that the viewers could scarcely perceive them—or the vision screens could scarcely record them.

"Maybe," Adrian said, "they come from places that radiate mainly in the infrared or ultraviolet." He was seated in front of the main forward vision screen, at a control panel whose purpose was mostly psychological; the computers handled everything except intentions.

Some of the shapes seemed to twist into another dimension and disappear, or the human eye was not trained to follow their pathways.

When they were close enough they saw that the ships were arranged symmetrically around the world, like the outdated concept of electrons around a nucleus. "Must be hundreds of them," Jessica said, standing behind Adrian, on her hip a three-month-old baby clad only in a diaper.

"None of them human," Frances added grimly. She was standing beside Jessica as if ready to catch the baby if it fell from its perch, even though, in weightlessness, it would fall gently if at all.

"No prejudice," Adrian said. "We're aliens among aliens, and we're likely to suffer as much from discrimination as they are."

They guided the *Ad Astra* around the little world, studying the ships and looking at the world they orbited with emotions ranging from concern to dismay. The planet was not much larger than Mars. It had a surface that was rocky in most places and in others softened, perhaps, by areas of sand. There was no sign of water and no perceptible atmosphere. It was a rocky asteroid blown up to planet size.

The motley collection of ships around it offered no evidence of life, no light, no exhalations of rocket or waste exhaust. The ships orbited in silence. The *Ad Astra* found an empty place in the shell—there weren't many—and eased itself into it. And waited. And waited.

"Nobody seems in any hurry to welcome us," Jessica said. She was slender and athletic and seemed as comfortable in weightlessness as under deceleration, but Frances was swallowing and the baby seemed as happy as if it were still floating in the womb.

"What is one more guest among so many?" Adrian said.

"You think they're all in the same situation?" Frances asked. She held out her arms for the baby and Jessica surrendered him without hesitation.

"I think they all got the same message, or a similar one," Adrian said. "Some a lot sooner than us, or they were prepared to receive it sooner, or they deciphered it sooner."

Some of the ships looked far older than the *Ad Astra*, as if they had been in space—bombarded by space dust—for centuries, maybe even millennia.

"If they got the same plans," Jessica said, "why are they so different?"

"Maybe they got plans suited to their own technologies and cultures," Adrian said.

"Or maybe they got the same plans," Frances said, making faces at the baby, distracted from her zero-gravity unease, "and read them differently, like people reading the same novel or watching the same movie."

"If that's the case," Jessica said, "we may spend a long time waiting for the welcome wagon. Whoever the others are, and whoever brought us here, probably doesn't have the same concept of hospitality, or of courtesy." She took the baby back from Frances. "It's time for Bobby's nap," she said. The baby didn't complain, as if it were accustomed to being parented by many different adults.

"I don't know why you call him 'Bobby,'" Frances said.

"We have enough Adrians," Jessica said.

"Only four," Frances said.

"And at least one on the way," Jessica said. She moved out of the control room toward the ship's living quarters.

"They could have longer lives than we do," Adrian mused, "and thus time doesn't have the same urgency. Particularly if they've been in this business for thousands of years."

"What business is that?" Frances asked.

Adrian waved his hand at the display of ships on the vision screens. "The contact business. The summons business. Bringing sentient species here. We thought it was just us, but it wasn't. The message seems to have been intended for any technological species. But if that is the case, why are they still here?"

Frances clenched her hands around the armrests of her chair. "I didn't want to mention it in front of Jessie, but this is like a Sargasso of space. Ships are stuck, unable to move, unable to leave."

"You've been reading too much romantic fiction again," Adrian said.

"All this may be the realization of poor Peter's worst fears. The aliens' purpose in sending the plans was to collect specimens, or to restock their larder."

"That doesn't make any sense," Adrian said. "There are easier and cheaper ways to get food."

"But not specimens," Frances said. "The zookeeper doesn't even have to send out an expedition; the specimens come to him and deliver themselves up."

"Now you're into the horror genre," Adrian said.

"Or maybe sick comedy."

"So what do you recommend?" Adrian asked. "That we turn around and go back? It's going to take a while to replenish our antimatter supply, particularly from this old sun. And even if we had the fuel, how are we going to face traveling all this way and going back without any answers?"

"Maybe we should knock on a few doors," Frances said.

"That sounds like human impatience," Adrian said. "And, as Jessie pointed out, we're not sure how the aliens welcome newcomers, if at all. Maybe we have to prove our good intentions by waiting; maybe a decent interval is an essential element in civilized relationships."

"Maybe it's hazing," Frances said.

"Let's give it a better name: an initiation ceremony. We'll wait a reasonable time, and in the meanwhile, we'll send out our antimatter collectors to replenish our fuel supply, just in case we need to leave in a hurry."

"I don't like the sound of that," Frances said. "Are there any other antimatter collectors in orbit around that weak nuclear furnace they have for a sun?"

"Not that we can detect," Adrian said. "But our instruments may not be sensitive enough, or the other collectors may not be the same design, any more than the spaceships that brought them."

So they sent their antimatter collectors to orbit the K-type sun and waited. And waited.

———

After thirty-five days—they still counted days and weeks and even months— human impatience being what it is, they decided to do something. Frances had said a week was long enough and Jessica, a month, but Adrian wanted to give the aliens more time. Finally he decided that five weeks was sufficient delay, for the human crew if not for the aliens. "It may be unwise to investigate the other ships," Adrian said. "Even if we knew how to enter one; even if we knew they were empty. And they probably aren't. They're probably filled with aliens doing their alien things."

"You mean, it would be like us going around to the other guests at the party, asking impertinent questions, like why they got invited, what they know about the hosts?" Frances said.

"That leaves the planet itself," Jessica said.

"But what is there to look at?" Frances asked.

"There must be something there," Jessica said. "Clearly the other ships think it's the focus of something, and clearly it is what drew us— and them—here."

Adrian's fingers moved over the buttons of the control panel. "I've been using our ground-penetrating radar. There seem to be cavities." He motioned toward the screen.

"Caves?" Jessica asked.

"Or tunnels. And scattered across that landscape"—Adrian motioned once more toward a scene that now showed, close-up, the surface of the planet—"are hot-spots. They look like ordinary rocks but they are hotter than their neighbors by one hundred degrees or more."

"If the aliens live inside, they would need to get rid of waste heat," Jessica said. "Particularly if they use a lot of machinery."

Frances looked back and forth between them, as if she were a spectator at a tennis match.

"And they would have to use a lot of machinery to live inside," Adrian said, "and those might well be radiators. They can recycle air and water and whatever else they find essential, but they can't recycle heat."

"So," Frances said, "they live inside. With a world like that, it makes sense. But how do we get in to let them know we're here?"

"That's a good question," Jessica said. "If they have camouflaged their radiators, it may mean they don't want to be found."

"But they brought us here—all this way!" Frances said.

"Maybe," Adrian said, "they want to be found but not too easily."

They looked at each other. It was another question whose answer could only be discovered by pursuing it to the end. "We'll never know," Adrian said finally, "until we make the effort. Radar suggests several places where the tunnels—if that is what they are—approach the surface. We can't just sit here; it's not just us—the rest of the crew is getting restless. I am, too. I suggest we go down and see."

Frances insisted on being a member of the exploration team. It would give her a chance, she said, to feel real gravity again. Jessica, however, was placed in command of the expedition to the surface because of her greater athleticism and quicker reflexes, and both Frances and Jessica insisted that Adrian was too essential to the *Ad Astra* and its crew to risk on this kind of mission. Since he was a reasonable man, he agreed, but he grumbled about not being among those who would experience the culmination of their long labors.

"If you're comparing yourself to Moses," Frances said, "remember that he died before he saw the Promised Land. At least you're still alive."

"And, unless we run into real trouble, there will be other opportunities to get our questions answered," Jessica said.

"And if we do run into real trouble," Frances added, "you'll still be here to try something else."

So, in a small craft powered by chemical rockets, they went down to the surface, Frances and Jessica, a pilot, and two sturdy engineers. They landed gently enough for a pilot who hadn't had much experience in small craft and none in landings on airless planets of this size. "We're here," Jessica said shakily. Frances noticed that she had been holding her breath. She had been doing that a lot lately.

They were dressed for vacuum, complete with helmets, and the voices came by way of intercoms. The surface of the planet was airless, and even if they found a way inside the likelihood of the air there being breathable, or, if breathable, not poisonous to humans, was close to zero.

They stood upon this ancient world, feet planted firmly in dust and rock, and looked around at the unpromising landscape: rocks, rocks, and more rocks illuminated by the feeble orange rays of the sun. Frances looked up at where the *Ad Astra* had orbited and saw scattered glints of orange where sunlight touched ships, probably not the *Ad Astra*, which had moved on since they had left it.

"Well," came a voice close to her ear, "what's going on?"

Frances started. "Nothing yet," she said, and she heard Jessica giving Adrian technical information about their landing and their surroundings.

Frances looked around. The landing was intended to be close to a tunnel that approached the surface, but she couldn't see anything that looked like an entrance. But then she didn't know what an alien would build for an entrance, even if it wanted one. Of course the aliens might have no reason to come out. Without the need for an exit, the entrance might have been permanently sealed.

"Maybe," she said impulsively, "the aliens bring other beings here to act as their eyes and ears. They sealed themselves up and don't want to come out, but they're curious and they have to find out about what's going on."

"Maybe," Adrian said.

"Or maybe," Frances went on, "they're agoraphobes who *can't* go out, and they need somebody to do the exploring for them."

"Maybe," Adrian said.

"And maybe we'll find some answers if we can find a way to get this thing open," Jessica said.

She was standing in front of a larger rock that stood like an obelisk in a field of smaller stones. She pointed to places where the rock had been chipped away, and other places where the face of the rock revealed a straight-line crack. "That isn't natural," she said tinnily.

"On the other hand," Frances said, "it may not have been done by the tunnelers but by visitors like us, trying to find our hosts. Why would they enter through a pillar?"

"Over there, then," Jessica said. "There's a cliff. That would be a good place."

She bounded over to stand in front of it. Frances and the two engineers followed more sedately. It was a good place. The rock face had been smoothed in spots, although this could have been the result of fault line splits from heating and cooling cycles. Some kinds of tools had been at work there, as well; some cutting edges, some drills, some evidences of rock melting. Someone else had been eager to enter—when the tunnels were built or after they were completed and the builders sealed inside.

Most of all, however, there were incisions of some kind that looked as if they might have meaning—like writing, if something even more cryptic than hieroglyphs could be considered writing. They fiddled around with it, the engineers muttering engineering talk to each other and Frances and Jessica taking turns informing Adrian.

They took pictures. They renewed their air supplies at the landing craft, and eventually they gave up.

———

Frances, Jessica, and Adrian studied the alien inscriptions on the computer screen. Adrian fiddled with the keyboard, bringing the photographic images up so close that their imperfections were exaggerated like the pores of Gulliver's Brobdingnagians. Here was a place that a micro-meteorite might have struck, there, that a flake of rock-face might have scaled away from the effects of alternating baking and freezing. On the other hand, they might have been the intention of the carvers. Clearly they had been created, and equally clearly they were indecipherable.

Hoping for a Rosetta Stone, Adrian had asked the computer for a comparison with its vast storehouse of images, including Peter Cavendish's spaceship designs and whatever else he had inserted into the database about the aliens and never revealed, but after thirty-six hours the computer had come up with nothing. *How could human minds find a solution that this computer, with its virtually inexhaustible memory capacity and its micro-swift data processors, could not?* Frances wondered.

"One advantage we have," Adrian said, as if answering Frances' unspoken question, "is imagination. This could be instructions for opening the entrance."

"Sort of an 'open sesame,'" Jessica said.

"Or it could be a threat," Frances said, "like the inscription on Shakespeare's headstone: 'Good friend, for Jesus' sake forbear / To dig the dust enclosed here / Blest be the man that spares these stones / And curst be he that moves my bones.'"

"You think they might be dead?" Jessica asked. Her eyes widened at the thought that they might have come all this long way at the invitation of creatures long deceased.

"Maybe it's something as simple as the inscription on a cornerstone: on this date, this entrance was sealed," Adrian said.

"Or: no tradesmen; deliveries in the rear," Jessica added, getting into the spirit of the discussion. "Or: emergency exit only—warning will sound."

"That's an idea," Adrian said. "It doesn't make any sense to provide instructions that nobody is going to be able to read. So, maybe it tells aliens who come outside, for whatever reason, where to find the right entrance."

"We're assuming that the inscription was made by the aliens who carved out a habitat for themselves inside this world when their air failed," Frances said. "But maybe it's just graffiti, like the names and initials carved into famous places all over Earth. This world has had all kinds of alien visitors; maybe the inscriptions are the alien equivalent of 'Kilroy was here.'"

Adrian put his hands together and pressed his lips with the triangle formed by his index fingers. "One sample isn't enough," he said finally. "We can't expect to come upon the proper spot in our first attempt. Let's try some other likely locations."

"In stories explorers always find alien artifacts or aliens themselves on their first attempt," Frances said, "and that is a good reason not to expect it to happen in real life. It's just a convention—a way to get on with the action."

"Not much action around here," Jessica said.

"Action is usually a sign that people have made bad decisions," Adrian said. "Frances is right: it's a convention, like the assumption that alien worlds have a single topography and climate."

"Unless," Jessica said, "like the moon and this world, they have no atmosphere to create climate and no water to change the topography."

So Frances and Jessica, the two engineers, and the pilot went down again to another site and another and another. Some places they found deserts of sand instead of jagged rocky terrain, some places, deep ravines and canyons cut by ancient waterways, some places, the charred remains of what once might have passed on this alien world for forests, some places, dead sea bottoms full of sediment and what might once have been bones that might have told them paleontological marvels had they the time and the paleontologists to spare. On the edge of ancient canyons they came upon what might have been the ruins of buildings, but none were substantial enough to tell them anything about what kind of creatures might have constructed them or lived in them; and beside the dead sea bottoms they found piles of blackened rubble that once might have been alien cities. Like the bones, they might have had xenological stories to tell and mysteries to solve, but all Frances and Jessica had time to do was to take pictures and move on. This was a world with all of the history of Earth—maybe more, since it seemed far older—but they had their own history that impelled them forward. They weren't explorers; they had been sent for, and they didn't know why.

Once they were caught too far from the landing craft when the sun set. The change between day and night was sudden, and they were wrapped in darkness. The planet was on the far side of its sun, and the sky, once the sunlight had stopped glinting from spaceships above, was totally dark. In the blackness of normal space, even interstellar space, stars shone; if they were cold and remote, at least there was light and the promise somewhere of warmth and life. Frances remembered the night sky on Earth and its seductive promise of other suns, other worlds, and the challenge of getting there. Here there was nothing but empty nothing, Milton's "uncreated night," Frances thought, and shivered. The darkness was like a premonition, a reminder of onrushing death, which even rejuvenation could not permanently disable; telomeres could be repaired but not restored. She looked down quickly and clicked on her helmet lights.

In the midst of the jumbled variety of this alien world that they had decided to call "Enigma," where underground cavities approached the surface, they came upon sealed entrances—or what might have been entrances. Near a few of them they found inscriptions; some of them looked like the first inscriptions they had seen, others, totally different, which seemed to support the theory, Frances said, that they had been made by other aliens summoned like them and expressing their frustration at a lack of welcome or not finding anybody home. But they took pictures of everything and brought them back to the *Ad Astra*.

"The Enigma remains an enigma," Frances said. Weeks since they had arrived had stretched into months, and they were no closer to the basic answers they had sought. Each answer only seemed to precipitate a new cascade of questions.

"We're bombarding the place with every frequency we have," Adrian said, "and we'd do it with Peter's energetic cosmic rays if we knew how to create and manipulate them. And we're listening to every frequency we can think of."

"Nothing?" Jessica said.

"Too much," Adrian said. "There are enough radio waves out there to fry a bird, if there was anything like that around. But we can't decipher any of it. The computer is chugging away like mad, but nothing happens."

"We could try to force our way in," Frances said. "With lasers or thermite wands or high explosives."

"Others seemed to have tried that and failed," Jessica said.

"And it doesn't seem like a rewarding strategy," Adrian said. "Even if our summoners aren't being good hosts and welcoming us to the party, breaking in isn't likely to win us any friends. And this far from home, everybody needs friends."

"Like Blanche DuBois," Frances said, "we must depend upon the kindness of strangers."

"I think we're finished," Jessica said. "We're faced with puzzles we aren't smart enough to solve. I think we should start back home."

"That's the mother talking," Frances said.

"I'm going down there myself," Adrian said. "I've let you two talk me into protecting myself and the ship, but I'm going to see that place with my own eyes."

Jessica protested and so did Frances, but not as vehemently when Adrian announced that Jessica would remain on the ship, in charge, while he and Frances descended toward the site of their first exploration.

When they arrived, the entrance was open.

————

Where a solid rock face had displayed only a few hairline cracks and the inscrutable incisions, a black hole had appeared, and Frances could see that the slab of rock that had blocked the entrance had slipped into a slender pit at the bottom. She laughed shakily. The sound reverberated inside her helmet. "Apparently you're Aladdin," she said to Adrian. "It was waiting for you."

"Unlikely," Adrian said. "It makes more sense that it was waiting for the team to return."

"Don't go in!" Jessica said over the static on their receivers. "It's too dangerous!"

Frances shrugged and then, realizing that Adrian couldn't see the gesture, said, "Are we going to enter?"

"I don't know about you," Adrian said, "but I didn't come all this way to stand in the doorway first on one foot and then the other. Jessica, I know Frances and I are risking our lives and everything else in what may be folly, but that's what this whole enterprise has been—risk and maybe folly, so one more foolish risk won't make any difference this close to finding out what it's all about. If we're not back in three hours, don't try to break in. This is not the time or the place for melodrama. And if we don't get back, you're in charge. If contact doesn't occur in another month or so—you'll have to be the judge of the proper time to wait and what constitutes contact—refuel and return with what we have." And he turned toward the opening in the cliff before Jessica could reply.

Frances shrugged again. "'Come into my parlor,' said the spider to the fly," she muttered and followed Adrian through the black doorway into what seemed, in the illumination from the lights built into their helmets, like a space carved out of rock and then faced with a dark metal or plastic.

Behind them the door rose silently and terminally. "Maybe Peter's worst fears are going to be realized," Frances said. "No wonder he stayed home."

"Peter's fears never did make sense," Adrian said. But he didn't sound convinced. "Let's look around. With vacuum outside and an atmosphere inside, we presume, this must be an airlock."

The walls were smooth without protuberances and the corners were rounded, like a culvert. The far wall was flat, but no amount of feeling around for knobs or switches or levers by awkward gloved hands produced any reaction. "Maybe," Frances said, "the opening of the outer door was an accident, and the inner door failed a long time ago. There's nothing to say that the creatures that did all this are still alive. It could all be an automated process that is breaking down, bit by bit. That would explain a great deal. We don't know how long those other space-ships have been in orbit…" She realized she was babbling and stopped abruptly. Too abruptly, she thought.

Adrian turned his helmet toward hers, and she realized that the same thoughts had been running through his head. "About this time," she went on, "the explorers would lift their helmets and sniff the air and say, 'It's breathable.'"

Adrian laughed. It echoed tinnily in Frances' helmet. "That never made any sense either. I'm afraid we'll have to leave our helmets on until we're back aboard ship, and hope our air supply holds out."

Light spilling over them told Frances that the inner door had opened. Behind it was a long, featureless tunnel, apparently burned out of the rock so that it fused into a smooth, shiny gray surface as it cooled, and perhaps with some luminescent material added so that it glowed. Frances felt as if she were in an artery of some gigantic beast.

"Apparently," Adrian said, "it took some time for the atmospheric pressure to equalize." He stepped forward into the tunnel, Frances close behind. Adrian knelt to get a better view of the floor. "No grooves, no apparent wear. But whoever built this must have moved a hell of a lot of people—well, creatures—and equipment this way."

Frances looked as far as she could down the featureless tunnel. It seemed to curve gently downward until, in the distance, the top seemed to meet the floor. "We've got—what?—a bit less than four hours' air supply? We can explore for a little less than two hours and then get back with a small margin of safety, and hope that the doors operate in the other direction."

Adrian looked at the doorway through which they had entered. It, too, had no apparent controls. "It would seem to register motion or maybe heat."

"If that's the case," Frances said, "it should be opening now."

"Good engineering would require some built-in delays to prevent cycling," Adrian said absently. "But the others know we're here. We should allow an hour and a half for exploration in case we have any delays getting back."

He started off down the unrevealing tunnel and Frances trudged after him. It looked as if it would be another long day. "Shouldn't we leave a trail, or unwind a ball of twine or something," she asked, "in case this corridor branches?"

"We have something even better," Adrian said, "a built-in mapper."

"Gee," Frances said, "the Cretans should have had one of those."

They walked through the gray luminescent tunnel, steadily trending downward, with occasional branches right and left. They stayed with the main tunnel.

"Nothing," Frances muttered. "Nothing."

"Were you expecting something?" Adrian responded, but he, too, sounded disappointed.

"Did I ever tell you that in addition to space sickness," Frances said, "I have a touch of claustrophobia?"

"Now is hardly the time," Adrian said, but he stopped. "We're getting nowhere. We need a vehicle of some kind and a longer air supply and maybe a bigger exploring party. I think we've done everything we can."

And he turned around and led the way back through the enigmatic tunnel to the entrance that now, Frances hoped, had become an exit.

Miraculously, it seemed, the wall slid down in front of them and up in back of them when they entered, and, after a suitable pause, the other doorway opened and they walked, free and unenlightened, back onto the planet's surface.

———

Four days later, the engineers had put together a small vehicle like a golf cart with a battery drive, a seat for two, and a space behind the seat for two canisters of oxygen. The outer entrance now was oddly responsive, admitting anyone who moved in front of it, including the cart when it was occupied but not when it was empty.

"Clever," Adrian said. "It can discriminate between living creatures and objects that merely move. That avoids random openings and closings—for falling rocks, say."

"Or it knows who we are," Frances said. "That would explain why it didn't open the first time Jessie and I were here. It took time to identify us."

"I prefer a simpler explanation," Adrian said, but refused to offer one.

The two of them explored the tunnels as far as the cart would carry them, sometimes exploring side tunnels. In the side tunnels, which were slightly smaller than the main one, something like doorways opened into something like rooms carved out of the rock by a process similar to that which had formed the tunnels. Sometimes the rooms were interconnected like apartments or sets of offices. But all were empty and unmarked even by dust or litter or scratches.

"They've got a great cleaning service," Frances said.

"I think they did it in stages," Adrian said. "When the climate began to change, through a change in orbit or a decline in solar output, and the air began to thin, they moved inside, first into the outer layers, then gradually deeper and deeper, abandoning the first habitations as they went."

"Or maybe," Frances said, "these were living quarters for the workers."

"Or as the central fires cooled, they moved closer to what was left."

"Or they're dying off slowly and clustering together in the depths for comfort and companionship."

Adrian kept up his hope of finding something meaningful even as each journey turned up nothing. Adrian and Frances took the first few trips, and then, when it seemed safe enough, Adrian and Jessica, and then Frances and Jessica once more. Once Frances thought she saw movement at the end of a long side tunnel, but when the cart got there she and Jessica found no sign of an alien or any evidence that anything had been there.

"What did it look like?" Jessica asked.

"Like something misshapen," Frances said. "Maybe with tentacles. Or viscous, like protoplasm."

"Have you been reading those speculative books again?" Jessica asked.

"I've learned a lot from books," Frances said. "Things I never would have learned if I had to experience it all myself."

"You also learned a lot that isn't so," Jessica said. "Me, too. People who read have active imaginations, and sometimes reading over-stimulates them."

"Too bad we don't have one of those *Star Trek* gadgets that detect life signs," Frances said. "And individual signatures."

"And transporters and magic wands," Jessica said.

"'A truly advanced technology is indistinguishable from magic,'" Frances quoted.

"So are wishes, and wishful thinking," Jessica said.

Eventually the explorations slowed down and then ceased altogether, not so much from decision as from lack of incentive. They had another meeting in the control room of the *Ad Astra*.

"We could go through this exploration business for a lifetime and never get anywhere," Jessica said. "Explorers on Earth fanned out across the world and still left depths untouched, and that took thousands of years."

"That's true," Frances said. "And there's only a couple of us who can go on any expedition, and an entire planet to search. If they don't want to be found, we aren't going to find them."

"Maybe it's a test," Adrian said. He was seated in front of the control panel, as he had been so many times before, but turned to face them.

"What kind of test?" Jessica asked.

"To see if we have the determination to persist in the face of discouragement."

"If that's the test," Frances said, "I think we've failed, and we might as well pack up and go home."

"That doesn't make sense," Jessica said, putting her hand on Frances' shoulder in a gesture of support. "We've made it out this far after years of effort that for you two began nearly twenty years ago, and through uncounted parsecs. What purpose would one more test serve?"

"That's true," Adrian mused. "On the other hand, we may be trying to judge alien motivations by human standards, and the fundamental nature of the alien is that it isn't human."

"But that's all we have," Jessica said.

"Anyway," Frances said, "there has to be a common denominator, a basic level of rational discourse, or all these other alien ships wouldn't be here, too."

"Yes," Jessica said. "There is a basic message, isn't there, in sending plans from afar to people who have the capability of understanding them? And of building the ship? There can't be an alien interpretation to that; it means: here's your invitation—come visit."

"Maybe it isn't a test," Adrian said. "Maybe it's a lesson."

"What kind of lesson?" Jessica asked.

"Well, they could have been here to greet us and tell us everything we wanted to know."

"Or," Frances said, "if they had been reading our novels or watching our TV, they would have got all mixed up with romantic entanglements, or differences between political factions, or confusion between philosophies."

"But it's not a TV show or a novel," Adrian said, shaking his head, "and we have to believe that their not greeting us was part of the message."

"Sort of a negative message," Jessica said skeptically.

"Not necessarily," Adrian said. "Maybe not greeting us was a way of telling us that there are no answers at the end of the journey."

"And the empty tunnels," Frances said, "that life is a quest, not an arrival."

"Exactly," Adrian said.

Jessica looked back and forth between them. "I find that depressing. We didn't have to come all this way to get a homily about existence."

"Would we have believed it if we had stayed home?" Adrian said. "I mean—I agree with the lesson in principle—life is a search for answers, not a finding of them—but believing and experiencing are different states of mind."

"But it's so—so—much of a letdown," Jessica wailed.

"If it is," Adrian said somberly, "then we will have to get used to it, and if we are able, rejoice in it."

"I think we should make one final effort," Frances said.

"What kind of effort?" Jessica asked.

"Attach a wagon to the back of the cart, fill it with batteries and oxygen canisters, and head down as far as it will take us into that labyrinth below."

A day later Frances and Adrian passed through the gates of Enigma and headed into the bowels of what had once been a living world.

———

They moved slowly but steadily through the main tunnel leading downward, ignoring branches, descending steadily. They had supplies of oxygen, food, and power sufficient for two days' journey into the depths and two days' getting back, unless something broke down. Of course eating and sleeping would be a problem, but they could survive, Frances knew, on brackish water regenerated within their suits, and occasional snacks of food paste from a helmet dispenser, and they could take shifts, one driving while the other napped, as best he or she could within an iron maiden.

But there was nothing to reward their venture as they drove deeper and deeper into the hollowed planet, and near the end of the first day Adrian's despair was only exceeded by hers. "There's an irony here, isn't there?" Frances said.

"What do you mean?"

"We launched ourselves into the infinite expanse of space, and now we're heading down into areas increasingly confined." She shuddered and hoped Adrian didn't notice.

"Maybe that's what's intended," Adrian said. "The science of our times: the galaxies and the universe on one end, sub-atomic particles on the other—answers to the riddle of humanity lie at either extreme, or both. I know you're uncomfortable. Maybe we should turn back."

"Never," Frances said, but she shuddered again inside her suit.

And they plunged deeper. The temperature rose as they descended, as if the fires of this ancient world had not yet been extinguished. They did not notice the change themselves, but the sensors on the cart registered the information and their suits' heat-exchangers worked a little harder.

At the end of the next half-day, the main tunnel ended in a blank wall; side tunnels extended on either side. When Adrian reported to Jessica, her reply was faint. "Your transmission is fading," she said. "It's having a hard time penetrating all those levels of rock. Call it off."

"Never," Frances said, but her voice was breathless.

"We're going right," Adrian said.

They took the right branch. After an hour and several more side tunnels to choose from, they emerged into a large room that was different from anything else they had seen. Something like dark windows broke the monotony of the luminescent walls.

"This is more like it," Frances said, but she knew it sounded as if she were not prepared for revelation.

"If it still works," Adrian said, and as he spoke the windows became illuminated. Scenes of a green world appeared behind the windows, slowly at first and then changing more rapidly as the world itself evolved through what appeared to be millennial transformations, flickering from window to window, with increasing speed until they whirled around Adrian and Frances like a fantastic kaleidoscope. The movement was too swift to detect individual creatures, only the vast movements of geologic—or xenologic—time. Gradually the procession of images slowed and the light faded from white to yellow to orange, and the landscape that had been green changed to lifeless gray.

"At last," Frances said. "They're communicating."

"Maybe not," Adrian said. "I think we've stumbled into a classroom. Alien youngsters probably could slow this thing down, inspect individual eras, find out what drove them underground."

"Then we still haven't contacted the aliens—or been contacted by them."

"This may be as close as we get."

Then the windows faded into darkness again.

"Jessica," Adrian said. "Can you hear us?

No answer came to their receivers. Frances felt a shiver of alarm.

The windows lighted up once more, one at a time. Behind each one was a creature out of Frances' worst nightmare. Some were spidery with long legs; some, winged with segmented eyes like flies; some with great mouths like sharks seemed to be swimming in water; some had many arms like octopi; some looked like ravening animals with four legs and big teeth; some looked relatively herbivorean, almost sheeplike; but most had no earthly counterparts at all, and the mind rebelled at trying to classify them according to human experience.

"I wonder which one is the Minotaur," Frances said, hoping that Adrian didn't notice that her voice was shaking.

"Perhaps more important," Adrian replied, "where's Daedalus?"

"Or Theseus. Unless that's you—Aladdin *and* Theseus. At least," Frances said shakily, "the aliens are showing us something relevant."

"This may be part of the schooling process, too," Adrian said. "Getting the alien youngsters accustomed to the idea that life comes in many forms, teaching them not to be repelled by appearance; or simply a catalog of creatures. No doubt there are ways to stop this display, and to explore the backgrounds and taxonomies of each of these creatures in as much depth as the individual student desires."

"Then they're still not talking to us," Frances wailed, not sure she could endure much more of this claustrophobic environment.

"No," Adrian said, "and I think we need to think about getting back. We've nearly reached our limit. We may never get any direct communication."

The final window, however, revealed a familiar face: it was a human face. It was Adrian himself.

"At last!" Frances breathed.

"Now I understand," Adrian said. "It's not a catalog of all the creatures who live, or once lived, on this world. It's a catalog of visitors—"

"Maybe that's why they never revealed themselves to us," Frances said. "They knew if we saw what they looked like we'd never listen to what they had to say."

"We're still primitive creatures," Adrian said. "We still judge a book by its cover."

"That reminds me," Frances said, "ever since we saw the alien ships orbiting this hunk of rock, I've been trying to think what it reminded me of: a school of predatory fish around a victim, vultures around a carcass, pigs at a trough. But I've finally come up with something more appropriate: those ships are like patrons of a library, and they're all gathered around the information desk."

"Then why are we the only ones not getting any information?" Adrian asked.

"That isn't quite true," said a voice they hadn't heard for more than two years.

They looked at the final screen. The image of Adrian had been replaced by another. Looking back at them was Peter Cavendish.

———

Frances was the first to speak. "Peter, what are you doing here?" She started breathing again, and hoped Adrian hadn't noticed the break in the pattern of sounds reaching his intercom.

"Strictly speaking," Adrian said, "he isn't here. Right, Peter?"

Adrian didn't seem surprised.

"Adrian is correct," the image said.

"You're what?" Adrian asked. "A computer program?"

"A bit more than that," the image said.

"A person?" Frances said.

"A bit less than that."

Frances fidgeted inside her suit, wishing Jessica were there, wishing she were not, aware of Adrian beside her, conscious of the impossible image in front of them. The image in the window looked at them with a calm that was uncharacteristic of the Peter Cavendish she knew. He was the man who had deciphered the first messages from space and published them as diagrams for the construction of a spaceship. He was also the man whose paranoia about the message had driven him over the edge of sanity, who had regained enough self-control to build a secret association of space enthusiasts, who had helped construct the spaceship and programmed its computer, possibly in response to alien instructions he had never revealed, to take the ship to the white hole that had led them—here. He was also the Peter Cavendish who had stayed behind when the ship left.

"Less than a person but more than a program," Adrian said calmly. "Whatever you are, it's good to see you again. We need some help."

"As for what I am," the image said, "I am a heuristic program modeled after your colleague Peter Cavendish, capable of learning, responding, and a limited amount of independent decision-making."

"Limited in what way?" Frances asked.

"Limited to fulfilling the objectives of this mission," the image said.

"Defined by whom?" Adrian asked.

"By Peter originally," the image said, "but modified by the inputs from each of you during the past two years, with a slight preference for those from Adrian, as the chosen captain."

"So we're really talking to the computer," Frances said.

"If you prefer," the image said.

"I'd rather talk to Peter," Adrian said.

"If you prefer," the image said.

"Maybe you can answer some questions first."

"Anything you wish."

"Like the genie from the bottle," Frances said.

"Why did you keep from us the instructions you programmed into the computer that brought us here?"

"I have an answer," the image said, smiling as Peter seldom had, "but you have to understand that answers about motivation are always conditional."

"The best you can do," Adrian said.

"It was my—or my programmer's—belief that the instructions the aliens sent for reaching them would delay the construction of the ship, and after the ship was completed, you—or more accurately, the crew—would be unlikely to start the engines if you knew that the computer was programmed to assume control of the ship and take you to the white hole."

"You never understood normal people," Frances said.

"That was one of my failings," the image said.

"We would have gone no matter what," Adrian said.

"I see that now. I am capable of learning, as I said."

"We could have chosen to override the computer," Adrian said.

"But you did not. Clearly I misread the situation, but then I was a paranoid schizophrenic, and I saw the world through glasses distorted by fear."

"But you aren't now," Frances said.

"A paranoid schizophrenic?" the image said. "No. Peter programmed me to be the person he never was—as intelligent as he but with a mind unfettered by apprehensions."

"Maybe you can tell me," Frances said, "why he stayed behind. He was the most driven of us all."

"Driven, yes," the image said. "But by fear of everything—of not finding what the aliens wanted, of finding what they wanted, of never being able to find a resting place between the two extremes. I was the perfect solution."

"I can see that," Adrian said.

"I don't see it," Frances said.

"He can stay at home, where he feels safe, and yet send out his alter-ego to discover the answers to his questions," Adrian said.

"But he'll never know!" Frances protested.

"Always the literal mind," Peter said.

"Unless we return," Adrian said. "But, of course, he's just doing what humans do: we have children to carry on our lives, to realize the dreams that we never manage to achieve, to answer the eternal questions of life and death and meaning."

"And the computer-Peter is Peter's child!" Frances said.

"Yes," Adrian said, "and Peter himself, in a sense—his mind sent out to explore the universe, to fulfill his destiny." He put his hand on Frances' suited arm.

"We understand all that," Adrian said, turning back to the image. "But why haven't you revealed yourself before? Why now?"

"I wasn't needed until now," the image said. "But you seem to have reached an impasse. You're discouraged, your oxygen is almost used up, and your mapper isn't working."

Adrian looked down at his gauges. "He's right."

"Should we get out of here?" Frances asked. On top of her claustro-phobia, the thought of being lost in this maze of tunnels was almost unbearable.

"As soon as we hear Peter out," Adrian said.

"I have communicated with the aliens," the image said calmly.

———

Frances put an arm around Adrian's unyielding waist, as if protecting them both against the terrors of the night.

"Why haven't they spoken before now?" Adrian asked.

"It took a while for them to learn our language."

"That's both too easy and too difficult," Adrian said.

"I don't understand that," Frances said.

"Adrian means that if they could send us messages, they should know our language," Cavendish's image said, "and if they don't, they shouldn't be able to learn it in a couple of months. But they didn't send us messages, they sent us images and mathematical formulations, which have few cultural relevancies."

"And they sent them everywhere," Adrian said.

"Everywhere there was a possibility of a technological civilization capable of receiving and understanding such a message," the image said.

"And how did they know that?" Frances asked.

"They had these listening posts, you see," Cavendish said. "All those white holes established near places likely to nourish intelligent life. And those who received the message and deciphered it and built their ships and came—each, in turn, has been exchanging information with the aliens as soon as the aliens could learn their language."

"But why are they still here?" Adrian asked.

"There is so much to tell, and to learn," Cavendish said. "All these creatures have histories and cultures and ideas and ambitions and art, you see, and all of these can be exchanged rapidly, but there is so much. So much experience. So much variety. So much art and science and philosophy.... The process could take several lifetimes. With newcomers always arriving, maybe forever."

"I can see that," Adrian said, "but still—"

"It's like a vast library," Frances said. "That's what I said when we first saw the place, didn't I? It's every bookworm's dream of paradise." Fear battled with expectation for possession of her face.

"Here I have to make a confession."

"Aha!" Frances said. Throughout her experience with Cavendish, she had wavered between blind trust and utter mistrust.

"The message wasn't received in energetic cosmic rays, as I—or rather my prototype—always said," Cavendish said. "It was gravity waves."

"Why lie?" Adrian asked.

"I didn't think anyone would believe gravity waves," the image said. "And they were so new and so unreliable. I was afraid people would think I was making it up."

"They thought so anyway," Frances said.

"Not you and Adrian," Cavendish said, "and you were the ones who mattered."

"Gravity waves," Adrian repeated. "Does that have some significance?"

"It will later," Cavendish said. "But to answer the other question—about it being too difficult: the aliens are consummate linguists. They had to be, since they have had to communicate with a thousand other species, and, what's more, their evolutionary development produced a species for whom understanding others was a survival characteristic."

"I can see that," Adrian said.

"Well, I can't," Frances said. "Sure, you need to understand others, but even more you have to understand the universe in which we live and work. Communication is okay, as far as it goes, but total communication can frustrate the need to get something done."

"These aliens don't understand that," Peter said.

"Frances means that accomplishment emerges from the frustration of incomplete communication," Adrian said. "Like art. Or science, for that matter."

"Then that's the point," Cavendish said.

"There's a point?" Frances said.

"Yes," Cavendish said. "The aliens want you to know that they are not the aliens you seek."

The image in the window flickered and disappeared, but Peter's voice in their earphones guided them back to the main tunnel and up its long incline until, at last, they emerged into the black sky and the ambiguity of uncreated night.

What is your substance, whereof are you made,
That millions of strange shadows on you tend?

WILLIAM SHAKESPEARE

⊢═⊣

Part Six

STRANGE SHADOWS

THE SPACESHIP ORBITED THE AIRLESS PLANET in the company of hundreds of other spaceships, each alien to the others. Inside one of those ships, Jessica Buhler felt isolated while a man whose body was thousands of light years away told his audience a story that was more incredible than the spaceship's journey to this far edge of the galaxy.

"The aliens want you to know," Peter Cavendish said from the computer screen, "that they are not the aliens you seek."

The screen had been set up in the largest dormitory so that the entire crew could participate in what might be the culmination of their long travels and the decades of effort that had made it possible. The space was long and narrow and cluttered with bunks and hammocks on either wall, but almost two hundred people had crowded in to see the recording.

"That's what Peter told us when Frances and I were in the alien labyrinth below," Adrian Mast said. He stood in front and to one side of the screen, his foot in a strap anchored to the floor. If it had not been for his serious demeanor, he would have looked like a sideshow barker, Jessica thought. Well, Peter was freaky enough.

She floated effortlessly on the other side of the room from Adrian, her arms folded across her chest, Frances in a chair on Adrian's side of the screen, with a seatbelt offering a gesture at security.

Why is it always Frances and Adrian? Jessica thought, and chided herself for jealousy.

"How can it be Peter?" asked one of the bearded crewmembers.

"I know, George," Adrian said. "Peter stayed behind. This is a heuristic program Peter modeled after himself, with most of his abilities and none of his hang-ups, and it has accomplished what we, with all our expeditions to the alien planet below, could not: it—or he—is in communication with the aliens."

"How do we know he is telling the truth?" Jessica said. The Peter she knew was capable of infinite deception.

"We don't," Adrian said. "But then we can't be sure about the truth of anything."

"Including the testimony of our own senses," Frances said.

"Then what can we believe?" a woman asked. Jessica recognized her as Janice Kenna. She was pregnant and had a baby in her arms.

"What makes sense in terms of our situation and the explanations that enable us to survive," Adrian said. "And maybe to understand and to manipulate our reality."

"But Peter could say the same thing," Janice continued stubbornly, thrusting out her baby toward Adrian as if daring him to deny its reality, "and he saw things that weren't there."

"And made other people see things, too," Jessica muttered.

"Peter's problem was his fears," Adrian said, "and they finally ate him up. Sure, he had his own reality, but we have a consensus reality—not identical for all of us but matching in enough places that we can coexist and even, sometimes, interact."

Laughter rippled through the rest of the crew; there had been considerable interaction in the past year, once they were free of the wormhole that had released them a year's journey from this spot. Being so far removed from home—Earth and the rest of humanity—had induced an odd urge to reproduce.

Some of the crewmembers were standing, anchored in place by an arm or a leg or a strap, like Adrian; others, like Jessica, were adrift in the zero gravity, wafted a little this way and that by air currents from the ducts. By now they had all grown accustomed to the sensations of zero gravity again, and the smell of each other and of the ship itself, worn by three years of constant living by several hundred men and women—and now children—thrown into close contact with one another.

"Data must be trusted until it is proven false," Adrian said.

"Or falsified," Jessica said. Her suspicions of Peter could survive almost any validation.

"Peter," Adrian continued, "or the program that calls itself 'Peter,' may be lying, although it gains nothing from lying—"

"Except an audience," Jessica said, "and maybe some recognition."

"That's true of us all," Adrian said. "But we shouldn't project our human motivations onto an electronic simulation. This is a computer program that lacks, or ought to lack, the feedback of audience or social response. Computer programs are capable of incredible feats of calculation but require precise and errorless instructions. Everything for them is on or off, true or false. But let us grant that this program may have developed the unusual ability to receive input and change it, or not receive input and say it did and invent a narrative that will satisfy the requirements of our situation; and let us grant that even if it is telling the truth the aliens it is reporting to us are lying—which may be more likely—I don't think we have any choice at this point except to listen."

"And evaluate," Frances added.

"And judge," Jessica said.

"All of those," Adrian said, "and then make up our minds what we should do with information that may be true, or provisionally true, or provisionally false, or clearly false. Because this may be what we have come so far to discover: why we have been summoned and what, if anything, we should do now.

"So," he continued, motioning toward the big screen, "Peter is with us now, as he has been with us from the beginning even though we didn't know it, a part of the programs that work for us and, although we didn't know that either, observe us. I think Peter has been observing our discussion and incorporating it into his reality. So, Peter, what have you learned from the aliens?"

————

A moment's delay stretched into minutes and Adrian began to shift uneasily in front of the assembled crewmembers.

"Maybe it wasn't Peter after all," Jessica said. "Maybe the aliens read our data bank and recreated Peter for their own purposes. Maybe he isn't in the computer—"

"That's an ingenious theory," Peter said, his familiar features flashing into existence on the giant screen. "But then you always were ingenious—and, next to me, the readiest believer in conspiracy theory, maybe because you were part of it."

Several crewmembers exclaimed at the apparition that they had not really accepted as reality until they saw it in real time. Even more shifted positions like Adrian.

"You all have doubts," Peter said, "and with good reason. I have doubts even in my present, paranoia-free condition. We are here in the presence of the unknown, maybe even the unknowable. I have only the communications of the aliens upon which to depend, and you have only my word that I am receiving those communications and passing them on reliably."

"We've already discussed all that stuff," Frances said.

"I know you have," Peter said, "and I want you to know that I am aware of all your concerns and that I would ease them if I could, but all I can do is to tell you what I have learned."

"We're waiting," Adrian said.

"I have received and stored a great deal of information," Peter said. "It is stored in the normal fashion, catalogued according to standard procedures, and indexed with appropriate words and phrases. The information covers not only the archives of the aliens, but also some of the archives of all the other creatures in the ships around you. Getting all of that information from all of the creatures and storing it properly will take time—more than the lifetime, extended though it may be, of any of you—and possibly technology that has not yet been developed, although my new substantiation has allowed me to perfect quantum procedures that may solve this problem.

"Most important, however, is that even based on the limited data that I have received, the information being accumulated is staggering, revolutionary, magnificent. It will transform human existence beyond anything ever imagined. The question that you will have to answer is whether human existence should be transformed, whether humanity can endure transformation without destroying itself."

Jessica's doubts shifted into overdrive, but Adrian anticipated her with "How do you know all that?"

"You always were quick to get to the heart of the matter, Adrian," Peter said. "And as usual you are right: I am generalizing from the massive quantities of information I am receiving, even as we speak, and its alien origins. It is an easy jump to the conclusion that this data will work the kinds of changes that I describe."

"But you haven't evaluated them yourself."

"Clearly not," Peter said, "and clearly I would not be a good judge of their impact on human minds and bodies, even though I can construct hypothetical paradigms to emulate human responses. But if the information is of the same level of technological advancement as the spaceship design and the antimatter collectors—whose influence on human existence we all know—then the additional information promises to—"

"Okay, okay," Frances said. "Get on with it."

"The aliens who are communicating with me say that their planet once was part of a solar system not unlike ours, as ours has been communicated to them," Peter said. "But it was located on the other side of the galactic center from where we find it now and about as far out on a spiral arm as our system is."

"If we're going to have to go back to the beginnings of the galaxy," Jessica muttered, "we'll be here for days."

"This was, to be sure, a couple of billion years ago," Peter went on, unperturbed.

"Good lord!" Frances said. Jessica thought that Frances was startled not so much by the scope of the narrative but, like Jessica, by its apparent duration.

"Then our galaxy crossed paths with another galaxy—a small one, fortunately, since one the size of the Milky Way would have caused much more, maybe fatal damage. This one created a few more supernovas and precipitated a few more black holes and disrupted a few systems, but otherwise did little except to prepare this galaxy for a new surge of evolutionary development, of stars and planets and, eventually, of life itself. The aliens did not know then and do not know now whether this outcome was by design or accident, but it seemed to some of them, in their state of scientific naturalism emerging out of earlier supernatural beliefs, that some unseen hand had flung the smaller galaxy into their way across the vast emptiness of space."

Jessica saw Adrian shifting position as if he, too, was getting restless.

"But that, in itself, was not the strangest part. That unseen hand, if an unseen hand it was, cupped itself around the aliens' solar system and propelled it toward the center of the galaxy."

"Impossible!" Adrian said.

"So they thought," Peter continued, "but the evidence, though slow in arriving over centuries and even millennia, was irrefutable. Their entire system was moving in relationship to other star systems and getting closer, bit by bit, to the galactic center. Where, of course, total destruction awaited."

"Of course," Adrian said impatiently. "So, how did they escape?"

"It's like a cliff-hanger serial," Frances said.

"The events took many millions of years, and their many nationalities and contending factions began to come together under the pressure of their inexplicable galactic journey," Peter said. "At the beginning they were fragmented even more than we are on Earth, which helps explain their skill in languages. And it was their skill in languages, as well as developments in science, that led to their staggering discovery."

"And what was that, Peter?" Adrian asked.

"They discovered the existence of a kind of matter that we cannot see or feel except as gravitational influences, a variety of dark matter. It was a large body of this sort, perhaps a part of the invading galaxy, that had captured the aliens' system and propelled it across the galaxy toward what seemed like certain doom."

"I can see," Adrian said, "that this account is going to take considerable time."

At last, Jessica thought, *he is seeing what I recognized some time before.* She wished it were all over, and they could do something—anything.

"We can't keep everybody here for hours," Adrian said. "Go back to your tasks, and we'll record Peter's message for later viewing by anyone interested. Frances, Jessica, and I will remain here to interrogate Peter."

One by one the others drifted away, some looking back with concern or disbelief or apathy toward the image of Peter Cavendish on the large screen and their three leaders in front of it.

Jessica thrust out her arms in a gesture of helplessness; the gesture spun her around until she stopped herself with a hand on the wall next to her and drifted across the space until she stopped near Frances. "What do you think? It all seems so strange and irrelevant."

"Like a creation myth," Frances said. "If Peter is to be believed, it started two billion years ago. Two billion years is a long time. We weren't even primitive slime."

"Long enough," Jessica said, "to dream up a story to explain how they find themselves on the edge of the galaxy."

"Scientists have speculated about the existence of such matter as Peter describes," Adrian said. "Shadow matter is what they call it, or, sometimes, mirror matter."

"I like 'mirror matter,'" Peter said conversationally. "Like Alice's 'looking glass.' You can't touch it or smell it or hear it—you can only see the evidence of it reflecting a world where everything works backward."

"Only ten to twenty percent of the matter in the universe is visible," Adrian said. "And only three percent is luminous."

"How did they come up with a figure like that?" Jessica asked skeptically.

"There isn't enough visible matter," Peter said, "to explain how stars move in our galaxy, the rate at which galaxies rotate, how much hot gas is found in elliptical galaxies and clusters of galaxies, the way galaxies and clusters of galaxies and the Local Supercluster move, or the formation of galaxies, clusters, superclusters, and the voids between. All those things require far more matter than we can see."

"It's all getting crazy," Frances said. "How are ordinary humans supposed to understand concepts like that?"

"If you want crazy," Peter said, "consider string theory, which imagines a form of energy with a diameter smaller than a quark and a length thousands or even millions of light-years long. Our universe may be only the three-dimensional shadow of ten-dimensional realities."

"That's as far-out as the supernatural and of about as much use," Jessica said.

"Maybe we should let Peter continue," Adrian said.

"That's okay," Peter said cheerfully. "Computer software has no sense of urgency. Besides, while you three have been talking I have been recording the history and literature of another alien species."

"What we're concerned with at the moment is the life story of the aliens who summoned us," Adrian said, "and when the story left off, they were heading toward certain doom at the heart of the galaxy."

"You can imagine," Peter said, "that the unseen hand that had plucked them from their troubled but normal existence in a remote spiral arm of the galaxy focused their concerns on gravity. In their place, we would have done the same, but for us gravity was a constant that we incorporated in our sense of the world, but never thought much about until Newton."

"And, of course, it wasn't until we progressed beyond recourse to the supernatural that we had any need for natural explanations," Adrian said.

"And so," Peter continued, "these aliens discovered gravity waves a couple of billion years before we did."

"Gravity waves?" Jessica asked.

"The mechanism by which gravity propagates," Peter said. "Newton assumed that gravity was a property of matter that existed without needing a medium, but more recently scientists have come to believe that gravity waves actually alter the nature of space itself, though minutely, and have developed instruments for measuring them.

"These aliens developed those instruments early in their civilization, and improved them until they were capable of measuring the smallest fluctuations," Peter said. "And finally they identified what they took to be signals."

"Signals?" Frances said. "You're pulling our leg. Or they're pulling yours, if you had one."

Peter's expression of earnest recounting changed to one of alert attention. "One of the other ships has begun to shift position," he said. His face disappeared and was replaced by a schematic of the alien ships orbiting Enigma, and then by a view of one of the absurdly shaped ships moving against the backdrop of space, at first imperceptibly and then more swiftly.

"What's going on?" Adrian asked.

The actions clearly were not in real time. At least the early stages of the ship's movement had been recorded over some hours until movement was discernible, but then it went faster until the ship began to dwindle into the distance.

"What's happening?" Frances asked.

The screen was silent for several moments until Peter's face appeared again. "One of the alien ships decided to depart," he said.

"Is that bad?" Jessica asked. Peter had always been good at sleight of hand.

"Do they know something we don't know?" Frances said. "Is something happening, or going to happen? What if all the other ships start to leave? Should we get ready to depart?"

"Ships come, ships go," Peter said. "They have to make a decision, the aliens tell me. Whether to complete the transfer of information or to take what they have and go home. It is a decision that you will have to make as well."

"Not until we know more than we know now," Adrian said.

"And you shall," Peter said. "The aliens had reached the point where they perceived that the gravity waves were signals. Deciphering the signals took more generations than we can imagine, even with their skills in communication, while their system was getting closer to the galactic center every passing millennium. And then one Enigma genius stumbled upon the key."

"The Peter Cavendish of his time," Jessica said. She could not stop herself from getting in a dig at Peter, even if this was an electronic simulacrum.

"Thank you," Peter said, "in spite of the sarcasm. Someone or something was trying to communicate with them. Eventually, after many more generations, translators began to decipher a message, or series of messages, and they finally understood that it was coming from that unseen hand, from the mirror matter that had entered our galaxy and had captured their world, and that the mirror matter world consisted of a different kind of existence, created at the time of the Big Bang, and that it consisted of at least one sun and one planet and intelligent creatures."

———

As if in response to their unspoken incredulity, the view on the screen changed to the solar system as they had approached it—the solitary planet orbiting the small, old orange sun. But now Jessica saw beside it another world with its own sun and its own strange inhabitants, shadows who lived and thought and acted as people did though only dark silhouettes. The vision lasted only a moment before it faded and she turned toward Adrian and Frances.

"Unseen hands! Invisible creatures!" she said, though she knew she was annoyed at her own susceptibility. "Why are we wasting our time on this kind of nonsense?"

"It is fantastic," Adrian said, "but much of modern cosmology presumes conditions remote from everyday reality. In time and if we had the right kind of instruments we could check the gravitational influences on this system. The mirror world may be invisible to ordinary measurements but not to its influence on orbits."

"But we don't have time or instruments," Frances said.

"Observation would be enough if we had time," Adrian said.

"I have been recording such matters as a matter of routine since we came out of the wormhole," Peter said from the screen, although his face did not reappear, "and my observations are available for analysis."

"What other records do you have?" Jessica said. Everything Peter said rose in her throat like acid. Adrian was responding with his customary, infuriating equanimity, and Frances kept trying to fit Peter's narrative into one of her neat literary pigeonholes, but none of them was the right shape.

The screen filled with a field of stars. There were tens of thousands of them like fireflies on a summer night, many more than could be seen from the Enigma planet, here on the edge of the galaxy, many more even than could be seen from Earth. And there was something subtly wrong with the stars: they were bigger, brighter, bluer.

"At a point in their history, the Enigma aliens—let us call them 'Enigmatics'—began to record their experience," Peter said, "but some of the earliest records have been lost or degraded. They were slow to develop spaceflight, but eventually they produced computer-controlled spacecraft that could observe the changes that were occurring in their celestial neighborhood and these files were created. It happened about a million years after their galactic odyssey began."

"Why computer-controlled?" Adrian asked.

"They are profoundly agoraphobic," Peter said.

"Though fortunately not claustrophobic," Jessica said.

"Whether they were agoraphobic from their beginnings is uncertain,"

Peter said, "but the experience of being removed from their original lo-cation and hurtled toward the center of the galaxy left them clinging to the familiar."

The view changed. Now it revealed a sun that seemed about the size of Earth's but a bit brighter. Gradually, as if a camera were moving in, planets came into view, a small planet, three gas giants, and then some smaller planets. One of the smaller ones had a familiar blue color, but it had two medium-sized satellites instead of one large moon. From the planet bright flares arose. One resolved itself into a small space-ship that went into orbit around the planet. The other flares also shut off; if they were ships, as well, they too might have gone into orbit. Then the ship that was visible began to move again, although without apparent means of propulsion, picked up speed, and dwindled into nothing.

"I don't understand," Frances said. "That's not the Enigma planet."

"That's how it looked nearly two billion years ago," Peter said.

"But there are other planets and two moons," Jessica objected. "Now there is only one world and no moons."

"Sacrificed to the greater purpose."

"My god!" Adrian said.

"Adrian is beginning to understand," Peter said.

"What greater purpose?" Jessica asked. "Why are all those ships tak-ing off? How are they propelled? Where are they going?" She felt a little nauseated, as if she had morning sickness.

"They are going to explore other solar systems," Adrian said. "As Enigma moved through this arm of the galaxy, it was gathering informa-tion about what lay ahead in the center of the galaxy."

"That makes sense," Frances said.

"And probably information about nearby stars," Adrian said.

"Particularly those that were likely to have planets," Peter said.

"How did they know?" Jessica asked.

"They were obsessed with the stars, you understand," Peter said, "and had millions of years to try to cope with their situation. They de-veloped orbital telescopes that provided a great deal of information, as well as these records, and then they had the guidance of their masters in the shadow world."

"How could the shadow world creatures get information?" Jessica objected. "They didn't have any connection with our reality!"

"Except gravity," Adrian said.

"Exactly," Peter said. "Gravity was their ears and eyes and noses and fingers. They not only made themselves felt by gravity waves, they perceived things in our universe in the same way, and perhaps with greater clarity, since gravity waves are everywhere."

"I don't know the wavelength of gravity waves," Adrian said, "but surely it isn't small enough to pick up much detail."

"It may if that is your only sensory input," Peter said, "and if you set up triangulations or interference patterns. But then fine detail may not be necessary if you are dealing with matter on the planetary scale."

"What I don't understand," Jessica said, "is what was providing the propulsion for the ships that moved off the planet by what I take to be chemical rockets?"

"I'd guess it was the Shadows," Adrian said.

"So did the Enigmatics," Peter said. "Their job was to put them into orbit. They didn't know what happened to them afterward. But they noticed that some of the distant planets they were observing seemed to undergo subtle changes."

"Surely the ships they were sending couldn't alter star systems!" Frances objected.

"No," Adrian said, "but the Shadows could when they saw that changes were necessary."

"Necessary?" Jessica said. "What kind of changes?"

"To make those systems more congenial to life," Adrian said.

"Why would they want to do that?" Frances said.

"So that they would be receptive to the next wave of ships," Adrian said.

"And what would they carry?" Jessica asked.

"Something that would encourage the existence of living creatures," Adrian said. "Right, Peter?"

"The seeds of life," Peter said.

———

Suddenly the pictures on the screen assumed a different appearance to Jessica. Now they looked like spermatozoa spurting out to fertilize a sea of ova. "The seeds of life?" she said. "That is about the dumbest thing I've ever heard."

"It's pretty wild," Adrian admitted.

"And the implications are even wilder," Frances added.

"What in heaven's name are the seeds of life?" Jessica said.

"In some situations, it meant preparing planets to nurture existence," Peter said. "Altering orbits, encouraging planetary wobbles, adjusting chemistries. But where planets were ready, the ships scattered the seeds of life."

"You said it again," Jessica said.

"It isn't clear whether by 'the seeds of life' the Enigmatics mean carbon compounds, spores, or actual RNA or DNA sequences," Peter said.

"What it means," Adrian said, "is that the Enigmatics may have been responsible for life in our galaxy."

"That's a staggering thought," Frances said.

"If true," Jessica said.

"The question is," Adrian said, "how did the Enigmatics come up with the knowledge and the means to do this sort of seeding?"

"They were simply following instructions from the shadow creatures," Peter said.

"All encoded in gravity waves?" Adrian said skeptically.

"They had many thousands of years to receive those instructions and to decipher them."

"That would make the shadow creatures some kind of gods," Jessica said.

"The supernatural but with a natural explanation," Adrian said.

"That, of course, is how the Enigmatics thought of them," Peter said. "And there wasn't much difference between the commandments of the Shadows and the injunctions of our own pantheons, except that the Shadows' were more practical. The Enigmatics had proof of the power of their gods: their entire system had been yanked out of place and was being hurtled toward what looked like certain doom, even if it was a million years in the future."

"There was that," Jessica said, "if that can be believed." She wasn't believing much of it.

"The Enigmatics believed it, and that was important," Peter said. "Moreover, they believed that the shadow creatures had the power to save them, or their remote descendants, if they interpreted their messages properly and obeyed their commands. There must have been many failures before something worked. And, of course, they had proof."

"So did all the religions we know about," Frances said. "It all depends on what you consider proof."

"They could measure the effects of shadow matter on their system," Peter said, "and they could record the gravity-wave messages and when they interpreted the messages properly, the ships they built worked, and they were propelled toward their remote destinations by unseen forces."

"All of which sounds like superstition to me," Jessica said. "That's the way superstitions grow, attributing natural processes of trial and error and eventual success to proper interpretation of a divine message. Who is to say that it wouldn't have worked if scientists and engineers hadn't simply built those things on their own?"

"And who is to say," Frances added, "that the Enigmatics in charge of the translation—surely there were only a few of them, like priests or sibyls—"

"Or Cavendishes," Jessica interjected.

"—weren't in cahoots with scientists and engineers who wanted to get their work funded by appealing to supernatural beliefs?"

"You're getting as paranoid as Jessica," Peter said.

"And who is to say," Adrian said, "that the original Peter Cavendish didn't create the plans for the spaceship we built and the antimatter collectors—?"

Frances shrugged. Even though she was strapped to a chair, the movement brought a look of unease to her face.

"All right," Jessica said.

"And who is to say," Adrian said, "that all of these alien ships didn't get built in the same way and find their own wormholes and end up here?"

"Okay," Jessica said. "I admit that I'm a skeptic, and I admit that there is some evidence for part of what Peter has been telling us. But I hope you also will admit that there are alternative explanations, and that nothing Peter has said in the past has been without subterfuge or double-meaning."

"I'll admit all that," Peter said. "The person who programmed me was a troubled man, and I can't be sure I am free of his paranoia, but I feel and believe that I am reporting everything accurately."

"One question I've been puzzled about," Frances said, "is if the Enigmatics scattered the seeds of life across the galaxy, why did the creatures turn out so different?"

"Even if it were DNA," Peter said, "environment and chance play an inevitable part in shaping the final result."

"Chemistry, asteroids and other cosmic collisions, eruptions, climate changes, crust movements, disease—" Adrian said.

"Even the development of intelligence and its combination with aggressiveness aren't foreordained," Peter said. "There must have been many failures, many blind alleys as in the evolution of humans, and many instances in which intelligence got embodied in some other form."

"Evolution favored the primates on Earth," Adrian said. "Maybe the equivalent of the dinosaurs or the whales or the dogs got touched by the magic wand elsewhere. Big, convoluted brains and opposable thumbs— that may be all that's necessary."

The screen changed to a blinding view of massive suns crowding the perspective. Then the glare diminished, as if a filter had been placed in front of the lens, and they could see some of the individual suns. Some were exploding, some were shrinking into nothingness, and some had their essence sucked away, in long, colorful streamers, into a halo feeding into a blackness beyond black.

It was like gazing into the mouth of hell.

————

Jessica stared at the images on the screen, trying to comprehend the titanic energies exploding in front of her, epic catastrophes, primal violence. Adrian's voice shook her out of her trance.

"That, then, is the center of the galaxy," he said. "One hears about it, one tries to imagine it, but the reality is beyond imagination."

"And this is what the Enigmatics saw as their fate," Peter said, "broadcast back from probes that recorded events here for some millions of years—a gigantic black hole surrounded by thousands of stars being torn apart by tidal forces and feeding their substance into the gravitational well."

"What did they do?" Frances demanded.

"Nothing," Peter said. "They could do nothing. Or almost nothing. They had used up their two satellites making spaceships for the Shadows and tunneled out their own planet for metals. They retreated inside the planet and waited for the end."

"And yet they survived," Adrian said.

The view on the screen shifted to the Enigmatics' solar system in the foreground, the violence of the galactic center in the background, small but growing larger. "Their hope, their almost religious faith, was in the shadow creatures, but as powerful as they were, the Enigmatics could not imagine how the Shadows could move an entire system. Maybe, some speculated, a single world, but what would a planet be without a sun?"

"And yet—?" Adrian prompted.

As the violence in the background increased, one of the three gas-giant planets loomed larger and then seemed to recede, first slowly, then more rapidly. The view drew back. The gas giant was moving out of orbit and hurtling away.

"The shadow creatures were trying to alter the direction in which the Enigma system was moving by ejecting mass," Adrian said.

As he spoke, another gas giant detached itself from orbit and was thrown aside, and then a third, and then, one by one the smaller worlds followed until only Enigma remained.

"These views must have been taken over a period of years," Adrian said.

"Actually more than a thousand years," Peter said.

The raging cataclysm in the background began to move slowly off center. "Another five thousand years passed, and the Enigmatics realized that their direction had been altered. The difference was only a fraction of a degree, but it was enough over the long millennia that yet remained to raise the hope that they would skirt the galactic center rather than plunge into the heart of it."

On the screen the central fury increased in size and frightening intensity until Enigma's sun faded by contrast. Slowly the maelstrom slid to the side. A sound like a discordant symphony emerged from the speakers and grew slowly until, when the galactic fury was at its closest, it screamed like creation itself. They had to cover their ears while they watched, on the screen, the Enigma world change appearance from blue to yellow and then to dull gray. The Enigma sun grew brighter and then slowly faded into orange, prematurely aged but not destroyed. The discordant symphony ebbed, and the viewers could once more speak.

"What was that?" Frances gasped.

"Chaos given voice," Peter said.

"You're trying to intimidate us!" Jessica said. It was more of Peter's sleight of hand.

"What he's trying to do," Adrian said, "is to make us feel what the Enigmatics endured."

"That's right," Peter said, "although it's all there in the Enigmatic records."

"I can't believe the center of the galaxy made that kind of noise," Frances said.

"Noise, yes," Peter said. "That kind of noise? Who can say? There are no ears to hear or minds to interpret, and no medium to transmit sound. And if there had been ears to hear, they would not have lasted long enough to register any sound. But there were instruments in space and on the surface as the sleet of radiation blew away the atmosphere, and not long after that the oceans and everything on the surface except rock. The noise you heard was the sound of radiation and of planetary catastrophe."

"Peter has become a poet," Jessica said.

"Epic events can bring out the poet even in a computer program," Peter said. "Compared with this, *Paradise Lost* was a family dispute."

"We didn't detect any radiation at Enigma's surface," Frances said.

"That was more than a billion years ago," Peter said. "In a billion years all but the longest-lived radioactives decay."

"And since then the Enigmatics have huddled in their tunnels?"

"And tried to survive," Peter said. "And tried to reconcile their experience with their faith in the Shadows. They had been saved, but they had also been nearly destroyed by the same hand. And they had lost almost everything. But finally they found peace in the realization that all this had been for a purpose."

"Like any other believer," Frances said.

"And what was the purpose?" Jessica asked.

"They had to pass through the fire, so to speak, so that they could continue their mission," Peter said. "They had seeded with life one spiral arm of the galaxy, and their next task was to seed another."

Frances, who had been staring down at her hands, looked up at the screen, which now showed a view of a jet-black sky loaded with stars.

"Our solar system is in this arm, right?" Adrian said.

"That's right," Peter said. "The reason for the Enigmatics' ordeal was so that they could foster us—and some tens of thousands of other creatures on thousands of other worlds."

————

"I don't know how much more of this I can stand," Frances said.

"There's only a little more," Peter said.

"Only another billion years or so," Jessica said.

"It is difficult to believe that one sapient species could endure for two billion years," Peter said, "but they had the Shadows and, for the first billion years, the threat of the approaching galactic center to focus their thoughts, and then they had their manifest destiny."

"That isn't the only thing that's difficult to believe," Jessica said, but Adrian placed a hand on her arm and stilled her angry motion.

"Surely they didn't use the phrase 'manifest destiny'?" Adrian said.

"Like everything else I have told you, it is a translation, and a shaky one at that," Peter said. "John O'Sullivan used the phrase in the middle of the nineteenth century to rationalize the American expansion to settle the continent. The Enigmatics used something like it to describe their obligation to spread life throughout the galaxy."

The view on the screen receded to reveal a spiral galaxy, its hub burning with massed stars, its bright, spiral arms turning majestically. It could not have been the Local Galaxy, Jessica thought, but the Local Galaxy might have looked like that if there had been a camera in some other galaxy aimed this way.

"The Shadows," Peter said, "instructed them how to create wormholes and how to harness dark energy to keep them from collapsing, so they didn't have to wait for ships to traverse the light years between the stars."

"Dark energy?" Frances said.

"Something is pushing space apart," Adrian said.

"Einstein called it 'the cosmological constant,'" Peter said. "He used it to explain a stable universe, and then abandoned it when astronomers discovered that the universe was expanding. Recent cosmologists have discovered that the rate of expansion is increasing and speculated about a 'dark energy' that makes up maybe seventy percent of the cosmos and repels matter rather than attracting it."

"Sounds like more of the supernatural," Jessica said.

"The more we learn about the universe," Adrian said, "the more supernatural it seems."

"Without dark energy the wormholes would not have lasted," Peter said. "With the wormholes, contact with almost every star capable of nurturing life became possible, and they seeded them and watched them develop, each in a different way. It was a demonstration of the power of the animate."

"As opposed to the power of the inanimate?" Frances said.

"Those are the two great powers in the universe, not the natural and the supernatural but the animate and the inanimate," Peter said. "The inanimate seems to dominate, to proceed down its inexorable, predestined path between primal birth and final extinction. The inanimate doesn't care whether stars explode and new elements are created, whether planets are formed, whether they are large or small, poisonous or nurturing. All that was laid down in the laws that prevailed when the universe was budded from the great potential for creation. But the animate has the power to intervene, to change the essential nature of the planets and the atmospheres that surround them, even the stars themselves. Always and forever it is the struggle of the animate's will against the inertia of the inanimate."

"That's all very pretty," Frances said, "but what does it mean?"

"And why are we here?" Jessica said.

"Why are we all here?" Adrian said, sweeping his arm to indicate the other ships surrounding Enigma. "Why did the Enigmatics send spaceship plans to us, and, presumably, to all the others?"

"Indeed," Peter said. "That is the question that drove my programmer into a mental institution and kept him from seeking the answer that he needed so desperately. And the answer is simple: the Enigmatics were asked to bring us here—those of us who were sufficiently advanced to intercept and decipher the message—for one last meeting, to share the data that each has accumulated in the long struggle between animate and inanimate matter, each in its own way."

"A gigantic information booth," Frances said. "A vast encyclopedia."

"But why do you say it is the last meeting?" Adrian asked.

"The Shadows can do much," Peter said, "but they cannot alter the path this system must pursue, and it is headed out of the galaxy into the emptiness of intergalactic space. The ability of the Enigmatics to maintain the wormholes is diminishing."

The view on the screen showed a darkness unrelieved by stars.

"What does that mean?" Jessica demanded. "That we can't get back?"

"It hasn't happened yet, and it won't happen tomorrow, or maybe next year," Peter said, "but within a few years they certainly will begin to fail, and perhaps sooner."

"And that's why one of the alien ships left?" Frances said.

"And why others will leave," Peter said, "but not all."

"Why not all?" Adrian asked.

"Those who continue into intergalactic space will inherit the full encyclopedia, and maybe the relationship with the Shadows when the last Enigmatic dies," Peter said.

"And when will that be?" Jessica asked.

"Those who remain are very old," Peter said. "And they are not well. The storm of radiation from the galactic center did not leave them untouched. Their ability to reproduce suffered, and those that were born were damaged. That is one reason you never met them."

"How many?" Frances said.

"Only a handful."

"How horrible!"

"Sharing data is not enough," Adrian said. "The Encyclopedia of all knowledge in the galaxy is a noble enterprise and a powerful tool, but—"

"You are right, as usual," Peter said. "There is a Purpose: to the conflict between the animate and the inanimate has been added the struggle between intelligence and the universe. The universe began in violence when no life was possible and will end in eternal darkness when no life is possible; between these two extremes, life emerges and develops intelligence. Intelligence has the power to contemplate, to understand, to imagine, to plan, and to act, and to frustrate the inexorable processes of matter. The Shadows created us as an alternative to chaos."

———

Adrian was silent. Frances was silent. Jessica was silent. Even Peter was silent. The end of their long journey had arrived and the answers to their questions, and they could not look at one another.

"So," Jessica said, "we finally have answers. If they are answers." They were not answers she could appreciate.

"This is our choice, then?" Adrian said. "To stay and continue to gather information? Maybe the critical piece around which everything else pivots? The secret of life? The secret of the universe? Maybe how to manipulate dark energy, how to create and maintain our own wormholes and become masters of the universe? Or to return home while we can, with what we have?"

"Or to continue with the Enigmatics on into the Great Dark," Frances said, "learning how to talk with the Shadows, learning their vast secrets in ways the superstitious Enigmatics could not?"

"If we can believe any of this fantastic story," Jessica said. Incredibly, the others were acting as if Peter's incredible tale was true.

"It is fantastic," Frances said, "but maybe believable because it is fantastic. Could Peter have invented something like this?"

"Maybe the Enigmatics invented it," Jessica said. "Oh, it doesn't matter. There's nothing to validate any of this. It's all airy nothing."

"That's my line," Frances said. "'...imagination bodies forth the forms of things unknown and gives to airy nothing a local habitation and a name.'"

"We do have validation: the scenes from parts of the galaxy that could only be viewed by something passing through them—" Adrian said.

"Easily faked," Jessica said. "Especially by someone as clever as Peter or the Enigmatics."

"The spaceship plans weren't faked, nor the wormhole, nor this world, nor the alien ships in orbit around it, nor the ruins and the caverns we explored, or the pictures we saw there," Adrian said.

"And yet there is no proof of the Shadows," Jessica said. "And no proof possible. Even if we determined the existence here of dark matter, or shadow matter, we can never prove that it harbored living creatures and that they communicated with the Enigmatics. We have to take the word of an unreliable narrator."

"Just like any kind of scientific hypothesis," Adrian said. "The explanation may be fanciful but it answers all the questions. As scientists, we place our faith in things unseen as long as they explain the data and predict the future without refutation."

"There is this great mystery," Frances mused, "and maybe we can hang around and solve it. Wouldn't that be something?"

"And maybe we hang around and spend the rest of our lives pursuing shadows," Jessica said.

"I understand that you want to go home, Jessie," Adrian said. "You have Bobby, and you and all the other mothers want a place to bring up children. That's natural, and I understand it."

"No you don't," Jessica said. "Being a mother doesn't mean you're any less a scientist or an explorer." She was a mother, yes, and she would protect her child against any threat, and struggle to make it a home, but that didn't mean that she would reject adventure.

"Yes it does," Frances said.

"Well, neither of you are mothers," Jessica said.

"But those feelings have to be part of our calculations," Adrian said. "You, Frances, want to solve the mystery of the Shadows—"

"No I don't," Frances said. "I just don't want to go home. If we went home we'd have to cope with all those people who didn't want us to go in the first place, and the people who aren't going to believe what we bring to them. And the people who called me fat and ugly all my life."

"You're not fat and ugly," Jessica said, putting her arm around Frances.

"I was," Frances said, "until I acquired character. But there's a third way. We could keep exploring on our own, maybe find a habitable planet and settle down to build our own world."

"That's true," Jessica said. "Going home has all sorts of drawbacks. Do you realize what kinds of people are waiting back there, the dolts, the stick-in-the-muds, the stay-at-homes, the let's-not-change-anythings, the Makepeaces."

The view on the screen changed to one of a blue planet fringed with white clouds, and nearby an oversized satellite.

"That's Earth," Frances said. "Are you trying to influence us, Peter?"

"Presenting the alternatives," Peter said.

"And what about you, Peter?" Adrian asked.

"I'm staying, of course," Peter said. "This is what I came here to find, the puzzle, the greatness. I wouldn't miss this for anything. I'm going to download myself to the memory of the Enigmatics and share in the mystery of the ages, maybe even inherit the intermediary role."

"So, whether we stay or go, we'll miss you," Adrian said.

"Not at all," Peter said. "The advantage I have over you material creatures is that I can go and remain behind. I'll leave a perfect copy of myself."

"You're right," Adrian said. "We can't both stay and go. But, Peter, it may surprise you to learn that we are glad you will be with us, wherever we are."

"If I were capable of being glad, I would be," Peter said.

"If we leave," Adrian said, "we'll never know the truth of anything we've been told."

Frances looked hopeful. Jessica felt upset and defiant.

"But if we stay, the chances are we won't know either," Adrian continued. "It is a mystery that took a billion years for the Enigmatics to accept, and even then it may have been a creation myth propagated by isolation, impending peril, and priests."

Frances looked quizzical. Jessica felt relieved.

"Our downloaded data is incomplete," Adrian continued, "but it contains marvels such as the data on the galactic center—"

"And longevity and inexhaustible power sources and insights into the condition of existence from a thousand perspectives," Peter added. "The wisdom not just of the ages but of a thousand ages."

"Do we have the right to deprive humanity of that?" Adrian asked.

"What has humanity done for us?" Frances asked.

"We are part of it," Adrian said. "And although it may be only a pretty story, the concept of intelligence struggling against blind matter captures my imagination. We must offer humanity a chance to be part of it, to make a difference."

"It's only a story," Frances said.

"It's by stories we define ourselves," Adrian said. "Humanity is a story, science is a story, all of us are stories, and we write new ones for ourselves every day. How will this story end?"

Jessica looked from Adrian to Frances and back again. Frances, she thought, whatever she said, wanted to return, and Adrian, whatever he said, wanted to stay. She loved him, and loved Frances, too; he was capable of drifting away into silent space, pursuing his own thoughts, but they were generous thoughts, great thoughts maybe, and capable, also, of being with her more than any man she had ever known, only occasionally, but they were special occasions. "Maybe there will be celebration when we return," she said.

"And resentment and hatred and disbelief in anything we say," Frances added.

"All of that," Adrian agreed. "If we return, we will have to proceed cautiously, releasing our information slowly as humanity is capable of receiving it."

"That might take millennia," Frances said.

"If Peter is right and we can apply the Enigmatics' longevity processes to ourselves, we may have that long," Adrian said. "The struggle may be endless, true, but maybe we can prevail. Maybe intelligence can reshape the universe, can stop its long slide into oblivion. Or if not us, then maybe our descendants will succeed. Or if not our descendants, then the intelligences they might create."

"Then you are determined to return?" Frances said.

"I'm only one," Adrian said. "We will have to ask the rest of the crew."

"They're like me," Jessica said. "They'll want to return."

"And if they didn't," Frances said, "Adrian would convince them. You're a persuasive man, Adrian. You have persuaded me. I hate humanity, but I will learn to love it again for your sake."

So, Jessica thought, they would return with their story, a sequel to Peter's credulous account of alien contact, and the kind of story would depend upon the way they told it—a contemporary novel of existential despair, an epic that defines a people, a revelation that becomes sacred text, a fantasy that feeds ancient yearnings, an encyclopedia to implement almost every human aspiration, or a how-to volume for reshaping the universe. Or maybe all of them.

Six months later the *Ad Astra* broke loose from orbit and headed back toward the star-strewn galaxy to begin its long journey home.